The Blac... Presents

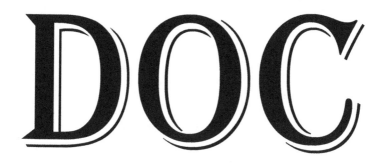

A Novel By
Jimmy DaSaint

DOC

Published by DASAINT ENTERTAINMENT
Po Box 97 Bala Cynwyd, PA 19004
Website: www.dasaintentertainment.com

"For there is not a just man on earth who does good and does not sin."

-Ecclesiastes 7:20

"Come to me my child. Come to me my child. Trust me. I will not cause you any harm," the Devil said.

Chapter 1
1968
Lancaster, PA

Inside of his bedroom, Randolph could hear the yelling and cursing which flew from his stepfather's mouth. His mother's pleading had been ignored as she continued to be ferociously beaten by her abusive husband. For six-year-old Randolph, the abuse had become a part of his daily life events. He knew every profane word there was and often he thought his mother's name should have been, Bitch, because his stepfather referenced her as such so frequently.

This blended family consisted of Randolph, Laurie, John, and Marabella. Randolph, who was called Randy by his parents, was the oldest child. His two year old sister Laurie was his only sibling; and together they shared a small bedroom in the back of the house. John Patterson was Randy's destructive and abusive stepfather. He was a large man who stood 6'4 inches tall and he weighed over three hundred pounds. He worked as a foreman at a local construction site and had a habit of beating his lovely wife; Marabella Patterson.

Randy's mother had been married to John for two years. Her first husband, Randy's biological father, had been killed in the Vietnam War. She was now a stay at home mom and did an excellent job at cleaning the house and making sure the kids were managed; as well as always having food prepared when her husband came home. Even when she did her best the beatings were just a part of her marriage.

Marabella was quite a beauty. She was petite and had the skin of a porcelain doll with blue piercing eyes. Her hair was blonde and she kept it short, and she had a long, yet sleek, nose that fit her face. Anyone who laid

eyes upon her was instantly consumed with her beauty; but she herself had never given too much thought about her looks. Her mind was always consumed with two things. One kept her in constant fear and the other gave her focus. Her abusive husband put the fear of God in her, and her love for God and the respect she had for his word kept her in the home with the man that had her in constant bondage.

She was a very religious woman and never questioned the word of The Holy Bible. She read the book daily and did her best to have her children stay living in the word. She wanted to protect them and their souls, but often she found herself trying to save Randy from the hands of her husband. John couldn't stand Randy and every time he had a misstep he'd punish him. He loved to hit on him and even though Randy tried to stay inconspicuous, there was just no hiding from his stepfather. And his stepfather wouldn't just beat him, he'd hit him in the head with the thickest belt in the house, and often wouldn't quit until Randy bled.

John was rough to the core. He seemed angry about any and everything. The only times he enjoyed himself and showed a softer side was when he had sex, when his lips were attached to the bottle, and when he saw his precious daughter Laurie; who put a sparkle in her father's eyes. She made him feel as if he had created the best and most beautiful child in the world and he couldn't have been prouder. He felt like she was the only person in the world he needed and he didn't hesitate to tell his wife and stepson exactly how he felt about them taking up space in his house.

"Bitch why the hell ain't this dirty house cleaned," John yelled at his wife before smacking her to the floor. "I did," she said, as she wiped the blood that was now running from her nose. "Well it damn sure don't look

clean! Get up and clean up this goddamn house," he demanded. "And get that stupid ass son of yours to help out to," he continued, as the smell of vodka reeked from his pores.

Marabella slowly stood up and walked over to the door. "Do you want to eat," she asked softly. "No! Just clean up this filthy ass house like I said," her husband shouted as he sat down on the edge of the bed.

Marabella quickly rushed out of the room before her husband wanted to beat her some more for asking him something he hadn't requested. She knew it would be fifteen minutes or less before he was knocked out on the bed, but based on how he smelled she doubted if he would last ten minutes; but still she knew it was best to get out of his way. When she walked out of her bedroom Randy followed her downstairs into the kitchen.

He immediately noticed the bruising on his mother's face and her bloody nose. Even at the young age of six he was in tune with the pain his mother endured, and he knew it was wrong for his stepfather to put his hands on her. He had hatred in his heart for John and he often thought about killing him.

Randy was no fool and his mind could be used as a deadly weapon. At the age of four he had been considered a child prodigy. His doctor noticed his ability when he asked Randy to place the most difficult puzzles together; not only did he complete them but he accomplished the tasks in a very short time period. His doctor called out a few specialists to study Randy and they were amazed at the young child's abilities. They wanted Randy to be placed into a school for advanced children but John would not hear of it. Randy's doctor was very agitated with John and called him to convince him that Randy needed to be enrolled. "One day that boy could be a great doctor. He is highly intelligent. Don't hold him back," the doctor

pleaded. John didn't care what the doctor said and he replied, "There's nothing special about Randy and that's that."

Everyone knew who ran their household so the doctor didn't bother asking Marabella again. The decision had been made. To supplement his thirst of knowledge, Marabella provided Randy with books and math lessons as often as she could. She even noticed that he could read the newspaper so she made sure to have at least one for him weekly. She loved her son and was very proud of him, even if her husband wasn't.

"Are you okay mother," Randy asked, as they sat down at the kitchen table. "Yes, I'm fine honey," she said, trying to give him a reassuring smile. "I hate him," Randy yelled. "Don't say that about your father Randy," Marbella corrected him. "But he's not my father! My father is dead! He's Laurie's father not mine," he screamed. "But he takes care of us all. So don't you ever say that again, you hear me? You mind your father," his mother said, staring into his hatred filled eyes.

Randy respected his mother and even though he didn't want to agree with her, he never wanted to hurt her by being disrespectful toward her. She was his everything and showed him a kindness he got from no other.

"Now do you see why I want you to become a doctor one day," his mother said, as she tried to quickly change the subject. "Yes mother. So I can be successful," Randy said. "That's right. And I want you to get as far away from Lancaster Pennsylvania as possible. It's nothing here for you. You need to make it in one of the big cities; maybe even in New York. You have the mind for it. Maybe even Washington or Philadelphia."

Randy nodded his head in agreement. He comprehended everything his mother had said and even what she hadn't spoken. He knew he had to get away from

the clutches of his stepfather. He had to stay in his books and to make something of himself. There was no hope for him in that home. Each day he and his mother walked on eggshells and he knew that was not the life he wanted, nor was it the life he would have to endure forever. He had other ans.

About an hour later, after they had cleaned up the downstairs of their home, Randy cut off all the lights and the two of them made their way upstairs. Randy went into his bedroom and his mother went in her room to check on her husband. John was knocked out across the bed and his vodka infused aroma filled the air. Marabella sat next to her husband and pulled off his dirty boots. Then she removed his clothing and silently lay beside him. As his loud snores echoed throughout the room, she began to weep silently. This was not the life she wanted for her or the children.

Down the hall, Randy was unable to sleep. His young mind was racing. In the darkness of the night he stood overtop his sister's crib as he watched her sleep. He hated this young child and felt no connection to her. The only thing he hated more than her was her cruel and coldhearted father. The thought of killing her crept into his mind. He wanted to but he hadn't figured out the best way to do it; and how to make it look like an accident.

"I hate you and one day you'll pay," he whispered to his sister before getting into his bed to lie down.

Chapter 2
Three Days Later

Lancaster Pennsylvania is located in the South Central section of the State; it's only 7.5 square feet with a population of about 58,000. Randy had been born and raised in the small town but his parents had migrated from a much smaller town in West Virginia.

Inside of his classroom Randy started to think about bigger cities and his life. He wanted to be around lots of people and safe from the abuse he had to bear. He pulled out a small dictionary, which was quickly becoming his favorite book, and he began to read it. His mother had purchased the used tool from a thrift shop. She promised him that the words in the book would take him beyond their town and onto bigger and better things. Every day he would read the dictionary because he believed his mother's promise. He didn't care how long it would take him; he was not going to be stuck in his small town.

Randy was the brightest child in his second grade class. He was the teacher's pet and the favoritism that she showered upon him caused a rift between him and the other students. He was teased; especially by the girls for wearing hand-me-down clothes and shoes. Randy disliked most of the kids in his classroom and at the top of his list was Sharon Carter. She sat next to him and made his classroom experience feel like nothing less than a bully's playground.

While he read from his dictionary, Randy noticed Sandy standing up from her chair. She began to walk behind him as the teacher stepped out of the room and left the classroom unattended. Sharon quickly bent down and tied his shoelaces to his desk. Randy had seen her bend down but he kept reading his book- hoping she had

wandered elsewhere. When he took his eyes away from his beloved book, Sharon was back in her seat.

Moments later the teacher walked back into the classroom and said, "Okay class, let's get ready for lunch." Randy placed his book inside of his desk and then he stood up. When he tried to walk away from his desk he fell back into his seat, barely missing the floor. The class erupted with laughter as they saw him struggling to free himself from his seat. The small wooden desk fell over and this caused the children to laugh at him even harder. Randy was filled with embarrassment. Sharon had done this to him before and he was tired of her picking on him.

"Are you okay Randolph," Mrs. Washington said as she rushed over to help untie his shoelaces from the desk. "Yes, I'm fine," Randy said, as he stood up. He walked out of the classroom and followed his classmates to the lunchroom. He was filled with anger but refused to let anyone see his emotions. He knew that he had to control his feelings because when he took his revenge he didn't want anyone to remember him lashing out. Sharon would pay. She had been a thorn in his side and never gave him a break from her ruthless pranks. He sat alone and ate his lunch and he never uttered a word.

After school he walked home. His house was only a few blocks away and since the town was known for safety, and everybody knew pretty much everyone in their neighborhood, no one worried about the children walking home alone.

When Randy approached his front door, the fear that often greeted him had arrived. His stepfather's truck was parked out in front; which meant the fear stemmed from knowing the man who had no regards for his life, wellbeing, or his happiness was already there. When he walked in he saw his mother on her knees scrubbing the floor. His stepfather was sitting in his favorite chair

holding his precious daughter Laurie, and giving her kisses; this was one of the only times that Randy would see that man smile.

"Randy come here now," his stepfather screamed out to him as he tried to walk pass unnoticed. "Yes father," Randy said as he approached. "I want you to clean up that dirty ass room of yours. Then take the trash out and feed the dog. Now go hurry up so you can help your mother scrub these filthy floors. I don't want my baby-girl walking on these nasty floors," he demanded. "Yes father," Randy said, as he rushed to put away his book bag.

Randy walked into the kitchen and held his head low. He couldn't stand the sight of that man. Why did he have to be so mean? "Why couldn't his daughter walk on the floors, they weren't dirty," he thought to himself. Things were boiling over. He was tired of the hurt, the pain and the skeletons in the closet. There were a lot of dark secrets living inside of their home, some that maybe not even his mother had known about. However; things done in the dark often have a way of coming out into the light…and if not Karma surely will pay you a visit.

with humiliation. What his stepfather was doing to him wasn't right and he knew it. He was living in a house where one moment he could be beaten and then the next he would be molested. He was sick. He was tired and had no one to save him.

"One day I'm going to hurt you, just like you hurt me," Randy said to himself as he tried his best to wipe off before going to sleep.

When John walked back into his bedroom he climbed into the bed with his wife. It took him no time to fall asleep and within minutes he was snoring. As he slept, Marabella lay there as the tears escaped her eyes. She had heard her son's suffocated screams, but how could she interfere. She didn't know what to say to her husband and she thought if she even inquired about him being in her son's room he would beat her; so she never said anything.

In the quietness of the night she whispered a prayer. "God please save my son from my husband. Please give John the strength to overcome his demons. I need you…I don't know what to do. Please God, please Father see us through this and whatever you will may be, I will trust you and honor you."

The prayer was all she could muster up the strength to do because she knew she would never bring up the events of the night to her husband.

Chapter 4
A Week Later

Within a week, John had been to visit Randy three more times. He was filled with lust for the young boy and each time he returned he had gotten rougher. He just wanted to thrust himself fully into the small child and had no regard for the pain or damage he was doing to him. Through it all his mother refused to interfere and Randy was left to feel the rage and pain of his stepfather's sick appetite.

One night after his stepfather had left from out of his room; Randy got out of his bed and made his way to the bathroom. He tried to clean himself off and wipe away the stench of vodka and his stepfather's musty odor. Randy then tiptoed down the hallway and peeked into his parents' bedroom. They were both asleep so he made his way back into his room. He quickly walked upon his sleeping sister and stood by her crib. For a few moments he simply starred. His blue eyes grew black. Randy knew how much his stepfather loved Laurie. He knew what he had to do in order to hurt him down to his core. He wanted the pain he caused his stepfather to be so lasting that it would take at least two lifetimes for him to heal.

Randy reached into his half-sister's crib and grabbed the soft pillow. He slowly placed it over her delicate face and began to press down with all the might he had in his body. As he thought about his stepfather he became enraged and pressed down with more force. He could see John forcing him to kiss and suck his penis and he pressed harder. He would not let up. Even when her little body began to wiggle and squirm, he did not let up. He applied as much pressure as he could, as his eyes leaked with hatred.

Her young body had gone limp. There was no longer life inside of her. He removed the pillow and looked upon her lifeless face. He felt satisfied and he enjoyed the sweet taste of revenge. His enemy would now know what pain felt like. John would have to live each day in agony and that made Randy's smile grow even bigger as it danced on his face.

Randy sat the pillow down beside his dead sister and climbed back into his bed. He closed his eyes and felt as peaceful as he could. It took him no time to fall asleep and the thought of killing his sister left no guilt or remorse within him. The murder of his sister was his first and one of the best feelings he had had in his young life.

Chapter 5

The untimely death of little Laurie had the family struggling to come to grips with her loss, and as they mourned one member of the family would never be the same. Her father was merely inconsolable. The doctors determined her demise was caused by crib death and during that era it was common for many children to die in their beds, so no further investigation was required. John and Marabella had no other choice but to accept the cause of death and their reality; their beloved daughter was gone forever.

For John the only way he could deal with his pain was by hitting the bottle. He would drink so much that he barely ate and everyone who came in contact with him knew he had a drinking problem. With the increase in his alcohol consumption his rage grew, and the beatings he handed down to his stepson and wife became more intense and frequent.

For five years it was an unrelenting nightmare but Randy did not regret suffocating his sister. He always found pleasure in the pain he knew he had caused John and nothing would change how he felt.

As Randy's twelfth birthday approached an unexpected occurrence brought him some instant relief from the constant beatings. His stepfather fell ill and suffered a crippling stroke. The entire left side of his body was paralyzed and he could no longer care for himself. Bedridden and unable to work, Marabella had to step up and provide full care for her husband.

This was all young Randy needed to feel free of his abusive and cruel stepfather. He had never felt better and kept focused on what he had always loved- his studies-and excelling at school. He had skipped two grades and his teachers had written to universities about his remarkable

learning abilities. His memory was impeccable and he was a critical thinking. The lesson plans his teachers gave him never kept him occupied. He'd often ask for more work because he grew bored of what he was given and he finished his assignments so quickly.

Another change had taken place for Randy. He was actually in demand. He was known as the homework hero and all the kids wanted to befriend him to take advantage of his intellectual gifts. He helped his classmates with their homework or sometimes he would simply complete the assignments for them. He was well liked by the student body for his gifts and he had a good rapport with the teacher who often gave him tasks to do that the others students envied.

One day after school when he arrived home, Sharon Carter and her friend Carla were sitting on his steps waiting for him. "Hey Randy," Sharon said as she smiled at him. It was a surprise to see them and although Sharon was a very beautiful young girl, Randy's feelings of hatred had never changed towards her. He was not going to let her slim built and long brown hair make him forget about how she had tormented him.

"What do you want Sharon," he scoffed. "I just wanted to know if me and Carla can study with you," she asked. Randy smiled and said, "I don't see why not." Randy's mind went into overdrive. His arch enemy had practically landed on his doorstep. He didn't know what to do to her but he knew he would do something.

Together they entered the house. Marabella was upstairs caring for John and didn't bother coming downstairs when she heard the door open because she figured it was Randy arriving home from school.

"So why do you want to study with me," Randy asked Carla. "Because everyone knows you're the

smartest kid in our town," Carla replied, as Randy smiled at her.

They sat down at the dining room table and took their books out of their backpacks. "Okay, I'll help you two," Randy said as his eyes focused on Sharon. "Does anyone know you're here," Randy asked Sharon. "No, both of my parents are at work. I came straight here."

Randy nodded his head as a devilish grin grew upon his face. "Everyone knows you've got the best brain in our school and we need your help," Sharon said, trying her best to bolster his ego. Randy was no fool. He knew exactly what the girls were doing and he was okay with it. They had their plans and he had his own.

While the girls focused on their lesson plans, Randy walked into the kitchen and made his way towards the countertop. Moments later he returned and sat back down with them at the table. About an hour had passed and Randy suggested that he walk the girls home. Carla lived only a few houses down and Sharon lived a couple blocks away; so Carla's home would be his first stop.

As Carla entered her house and waved goodbye, the approaching night sky began to darken. It was getting late and Sharon wanted to get home before her parents came back from work.

"Let's take a shortcut through the park," Randy suggested. "You'll get home before your parents for sure if we take this route," he continued. Sharon heard shortcut and was all for it. She had no reason to doubt Randy; besides he seemed to know everything anyway.

"Did you hear about the dead cats they found in the park," Randy asked. "Yes, how gross," she replied, not realizing that Randy had been the culprit. The kid she had bullied, who she laughed at and called a weirdo, had slyly taken out his knife and was waiting for the precise moment to take his revenge.

Chapter 6

The small park was filled with trees. There was a small pond and a long dusty trail that extended from the beginning of the park to the end. On this cold winter day the grounds were uninhabited.

"Sharon can I ask you something," Randy said as he gripped the knife he held closely in his hand. "Yeah, what is it," she said, unaware of the danger she was in.

As they paused momentarily he turned to her and said, "Why me? What made you tease and torture me?" Sharon gazed into his eyes and she now began to feel uneasy. She didn't know where this was all coming from. He had just helped her study and was now walking her home, so what was his problem, she wondered.

"I...I was just messing around Randy. It wasn't personal. I was just playing," young Sharon fearfully said, as she watched his demented eyes.

Instantaneously Randy grabbed Sharon by her hair and began to stab her in the neck. She tried to scream but the puncture wounds to her vocal cords quickly muffled any sounds. Sharon tried to fight with all the strength she had in her body but Randy easily overpowered her. He even found it comical that she continued to resist him; so Randy let her go only to quickly recapture her then he continued to slash her throat.

Randy threw Sharon to the cold ground and began to stab her body; enjoying each moment that the knife entered her soft flesh. The thrill of killing his enemy gave him an erection. He started to cut deeper. Then for the fun of it he gouged one of her eyes. He held it in his hands and examined it before he placed it in his pocket.

Randy had stabbed Sharon over a hundred times. He stared at her corpse and was pleased to see the work he

had done to it. He was calm as he stood up and walked away as if he had not a care in the world.

Ten minutes later he was back home. Randy crept through the backdoor to his home and swiftly made his way upstairs into his bedroom. He removed his blood stained clothing and placed them and his sneakers inside of his backpack. He went into the bathroom and took a steamy hot shower before putting on his nightclothes.

Randy then grabbed a box of matches from the kitchen and then he went into the backyard. Once he had the backpack inside of the metal trashcan, he lit a few matches to the contents until the flame had consumed the bloody items.

Back in his bedroom he knelt down beside his bed. He thought of the joy his first kill had brought to him and then he pulled the deadly weapon from underneath his bed, along with a small plastic bag. He taped the knife to the bedframe underneath his mattress and then he focused his attention to the object in the small plastic bag. He had waited for this moment all night and finally he had the chance to see if his assumption was right.

He removed Sharon's eyeball from the bag and enjoyed the sight as he again stared at it. Then he opened up his mouth and slowly placed it inside. He swished the eye in his mouth as if he was at a winetasting and then he swallowed it whole.

"Now you'll always be a part of me," Randy said softly as he finished his tasty treat.

Chapter 7

A few days had passed before the mutilated body of young Sharon was found. The coroner stated she had been stabbed over one-hundred-twenty times and the town was outraged and filled with fear. They had never witnessed any murders and this type of killing was just not heard of; especially since it was a young child.

The authorities backtracked Sharon's last steps. They questioned Carla and Randy about the last time they had saw Sharon. Both children were not only helpful but quite believable. Randy was sure to tell the cops that he walked Sharon towards the entrance of the park but went home after she insisted she would go the rest of the way alone. This led them to believe that her killer had been waiting in the park for his prey. The sheriff contacted neighboring towns and called in a specialist because they thought they had a serial and sadistic killer on their hands. The entire town's attention was now focused on finding young Sharon's murderer.

Randy was pleased. He was now two for two. He knew he'd go undetected because of the knowledge he had acquired from studying killers and how to commit the perfect crime. Those books were readily available in the library and since no one was focused on what the young man read in his spare time, he consumed as much as he could on that topic. Randy was eager to kill and curious about the thrill he would get once he had accomplished his mission, and now that he was a killer he felt somewhat satisfied but he yearned for more.

Killing cats was nothing like murdering a human being. The feeling Randy got from taking another's life was euphoric. He felt high on life as his victims' last breath escaped their bodies. He knew this was just the beginning for him because he could not shake the urge to

murder someone else, but he felt as if he had to wait until he had a reason to take another's life.

With the chaos heavy and hectic in town and everyone focusing on finding Sharon's killer, Randy placed his attention back towards his education. He knew almost every word in the dictionary, and he could spell the words he knew front and backwards. Randy began to look into books on modern medicine, world history, and he studied psychology; but he got a bigger thrill when reading stories about famous serial killers. Two of his current favorites were Gilles De Rais, a French nobleman, who was considered to be the precursor to the modern day serial killer, and Albert Fish, who was also known as the Brooklyn Vampire; and he had boasted that he molested over one hundred children and was a suspect in many of their murders.

Learning was therapeutic for Randy and the library had turned into his home. The librarian watched as he entered the library and stayed to closing, and at times she felt sorry for him. He was only thirteen but the town had pegged the young man a weird character. They didn't bother him and they gave him plenty of space. He had no friends and all he did was read. She found this to be strange but never questioned him because of the creepy vibe she got from him.

Randy wasn't bothered by the stares or the whispers. He knew he was different and while children were saying they were going to grow up to be cops, doctors, of firefighters, he had his mind made up. Randy wanted to be a famous M.D.; and a psychologist who covered as a cold blooded serial killer.

Chapter 8
1977

Inside of his bedroom, Randy sat reading a book on human anatomy. He had become obsessed with how the body operated and wanted to learn all he could. As he perused through the nine-hundred page book, the sound of disco music played from his small radio. Even though reading was his passion, music had become something he enjoyed as well.

The swift knock at the door startled him as his mother walked into his room. Her frail, thin body appeared to be much older than her true age of thirty-five. Her blue piercing eyes stood out and Randy loved to gaze upon them. He thought they looked like real life marbles.

"Yes mother, what is it," Randy asked as he stared at her. She sat down on his bed and grabbed one of his hands. "Your father is not doing well. I don't think he's going to be with us much longer," his mother said. Randy was silent. His face showed no emotion.

"I would like us to pray for him before God takes him away," Marabella said. Randy looked directly into his mother's eyes and said, "Let him die! And if there is a God, which I don't think there is or has ever been, but if there is one, I hope he will punish John for all the pain he has placed upon us."

Randy's words stung his mother. She knew that John had molested her son but she had sworn she'd never address it. And her son was not finished. Randy made his mother see what had been going on in the darkness of the night.

"John tortured me. He molested me for years until he had his stroke. That stroke saved me from many years of his lustful desires. Mother your love for him is something I'll never understand. You know the sins your

husband committed but you protect him with your Bible. I want you to take that worthless book and leave my room. I hate John Patterson and there is no God!"

Tears flowed from her eyes as she began to choke on her guilt. She was overwhelmed and her son's harsh and truthful words had devastated her. There was nothing she could say, no apology she could give for allowing the abuse to continue as she stayed with the man who had stolen her son's innocence.

Marabella tearfully stood up and walked out of her son's room. Randy was emotionally detached as his mother wept and he refocused his attention. As Donna Summer's voice flowed from his small radio, he got back into his book. He was going to be a medical doctor despite his past. Now as he turned the page to his favorite chapter, the human heart, an unspeakable excitement filled his body.

Chapter 9

Randy was a loner. He had no real friends besides his teachers at school. Most of the students felt he was weird and if they didn't need to be tutored, they kept their distance. He didn't mind that one bit.

Randy enjoyed the sounds of disco, he dressed like a hippy; and was never seen without at least six or more books in his clutches. The kids at school all knew he had dreams of becoming a doctor and they nicknamed him, "The Mad Doctor." One day one of his classmates said to him, "What's up Doc," and from then on the nickname, Doc stuck.

Young Randy didn't play sports nor did he waste his time on anything else besides keeping his head in a book. His I-Q was tested and he scored 138; which was extremely high for a boy who hadn't yet turned sixteen. Harvard, Yale, Stanford, and Princeton Universities had already begun to show interest in him.

During this time another force was at work on the young boy. Puberty had hit and it was overwhelming. The urges he had for sex were uncontrollable and to put himself at ease he masturbated four to five times daily. He hungered to fulfill his sexual appetite but for now the Penthouse and Playboy magazines under his bed had to give him his needed fix. Even this proved to be a tricky quest because if the women in the magazines didn't have blue or green eyes, he could not ejaculate. The color of a woman's eyes had become another one of his obsessions.

Later That Night

After he had finished taking a hot and steamy shower, Randy sat on his bed inside of his room. He had lotioned himself down and lay his nude body under the covers. In an instant his sexual appetite rose. His penis was fully erect and he felt like it would explode. He reached under his pillow and pulled out a small photo of a woman. Holding it to his face he stared at it intensely. Then he retained the image in his memory as he placed it down and began to pleasure himself.

Once he exploded all over, he grabbed a washcloth and went into the bathroom to clean off. He returned to his bedroom feeling light and ready to rest. Randy then picked up the photo as he lay down and stared at the subject's piercing blue eyes.

"I love you mother," Randy said, as he kissed the photo and placed it back under his pillow before falling into a peaceful sleep.

Chapter 10
A Few Days Later

With a warm bowl of chicken soup in her hands, Marabella walked into her bedroom and sat beside her sickly husband. John was still bedridden and unable to care for himself. He was in need of Marabella's help and without it his condition would surely worsen. She had to massage his body, rotate his position in bed so he could avoid getting bed sores, as well as feeding him and helping him use the bathroom. Though her husband had caused her much pain and her son hated him, she vowed to stay by his side. Marabella's mother had taught her that you never leave you man when times get hard, that your marriage vows were sacred and that they were for life; and she was honoring them until he took his last breath.

Marabella propped a pillow under John's head and slowly began to feed him the warm soup. Each time he'd make a mess she would gently wipe his mouth off. This was her duty. In her heart she knew she was not in love with this man but she wouldn't leave him. He was broken and not only had the stroke caused him severe pain, but the death of their daughter Laurie had crippled him for life.

Once she finished feeding her husband she placed the bowl down and reached for The Holy Bible. She began to read a passage from the book of revelations. John was unable to speak clearly but as he heard the words he became overwhelmed and tears started to fall from his eyes. Each word she spoke penetrated his core and the demons inside of him began to awake in a fury. He tried to utter a few words for his wife to stop reading from that book but Marabella continued to read the scripture. She could not understand what he was saying but she continued. She knew her husband didn't want to hear the

word but he needed to hear some truth. It was a part of her mission for her husband to learn, hear, and respect and honor the word of God.

Randy peered into his mother's bedroom and smiled as he watched his stepfather being tormented by the words from The Holy Bible. He was pleased to see the man who had caused him so much pain suffering at the hands of his mother. She was able to crush John without laying a finger on him.

"Get that bastard," Randy uttered underneath his breath as he quietly walked away.

Chapter 11
March, 1977

Randy sat on his porch observing as his new neighbors moved into the house next door. The family was an African-American household, with a husband and wife; and their fifteen year old daughter Annie.

As the movers brought in the furniture, the young female noticed Randy staring at her. She causally walked over to him and introduced herself.

"Hi, my name is Annie. We just moved here from Philadelphia. What's your name," she asked. Randy smiled. It was the first time he had ever met a black person. He scanned Annie's body from head to toe. She was very curvaceous. She had a deep dark complexion and wore her hair in a long ponytail that reached the middle of her back. Her cheekbones were high and her eyes were a beautiful rich, dark brown color.

"My name is Randy but people call me Doc," he said. "Okay Doc. Can you tell me how it is around here," she asked, as she took a seat beside him. "It seems a little quiet," she continued. Randy enjoyed her directness and replied, "It's okay. Not much goes on around here. It's a small town and I'm sure it's nothing like Philadelphia, but if you like small towns you should be fine." She looked at him and sadly said, "Well to be honest I don't like small towns but my father moved here for work. I didn't want to leave my home because all my friends are there and I miss them."

Randy looked at her and said, "Well I don't have many friends here. I stay to myself." Annie noticed his blue eyes and could feel his loneliness. She was captivated by his eyes. They were different but very nice. She replied, "I'll be your new friend. Plus I think you're cute."

That was the first time anyone had offered to be Randy's friend with no strings attached. Any other time someone befriended him, they wanted help with their homework, or they wanted him to do their homework. It was a pleasant feeling for Randy to have someone approach him and offer their friendship; and for the young lady to say he was cute was definitely a welcomed first. Even though Randy wasn't physically attracted to the pretty young girl, he did like her openness and honesty.

"You like me," Randy asked, just to ensure he had heard her correctly the first time. "Yes, you're really cute Randy. I mean Doc. Maybe we can hang out sometimes. I'm the only child and it can be pretty boring at my house," Annie said, with a wide smile upon her face as she stood up and began to head to her house. "Sure we can hang out. I'm always home. If I'm not here I'm at the library but I can come home more," Randy said enthusiastically. "Great, I'll come back to see you then," Annie said with a wide smile.

Doc watched as Annie walked away. That was the first time he had been approached by a female and he enjoyed the attention. He stood up and walked inside as his smile lit up the entire house.

Chapter 12
May, 1977

A few months passed and Doc and Annie's friendship blossomed. Each day after school they would spend time together and they were becoming the best of friends. People stared at the odd couple but the duo paid no attention to the wayward looks. They were friends and weren't going to let any whispers or the prejudices of others divide them.

The pair spent a good portion of their time studying and then they would watch their favorite TV sitcoms; Happy Days, Lavern & Shirley, and Three's Company. Then at night they would speak on the phones for as long as their parents would allow.

Doc always wanted to talk about the books he had read and becoming a doctor, but Annie was the complete opposite. She hated school and rules. She didn't care about anything except getting her way and having a good time. She was a spoiled brat and her parents couldn't control her. It was one of the contributing factors that led to her parents moving to this small town. They wanted to try and keep Annie away from the pull of the big city; even though they knew she was the ring leader.

While sitting inside of Randy's bedroom one night, the two watched an episode of Good Times. Annie went inside of her pocket and to Doc's surprise; she pulled out a small quantity of reefa and rolled up a joint.

"What's that," Doc asked. "It's marijuana. I stole it from my dad," Annie said. "I don't smoke that stuff," Doc said. "Well tonight you will smoke this joint. It's good stuff. It makes me feel good and I use it all the time," Annie said as she took her matches and lit up her joint.

Doc watched as Annie inhaled the herbal treat. He then gazed upon the smoke as Annie exhaled the clouds of

smoke out of her mouth. She took two more pulls before passing the joint to Doc. He didn't want to smoke but he also didn't want to be upstaged by a girl.

Doc placed the joint to his lips and began to inhale the herbs into his virgin lungs. Instantly he began to cough uncontrollably. He was embarrassed but he decided that he was going to try again. As he pulled on the joint twice more, he coughed again but this time he had a better grip on the technique. When they had finished the joint they were lifted.

"Didn't I tell you that you'd feel good," Annie asked Doc. He nodded his head in agreement. He was high and feeling groovy. He felt light and happy; a combination he didn't feel often. Then without warning Annie leaned over and kissed Doc. He was caught off guard and didn't know what to say or do. "I love you Doc. You're a little strange sometimes but I wouldn't change a thing about you," Annie said.

Doc still had nothing to say. He was lost for words. He really liked Annie. Besides his mother she was the only person in his life that treated him good. Doc truly cared for his friend Annie.

"I love you too," Doc finally said. "Cool," Annie said, as she reached out her hand towards Doc. "Best friends for life," Annie said, as she extended her pinky finger towards Doc's hand. "Yes, best friends for life," Doc said as they pinky swore. In that moment they made a promise to always have each other's back. They knew that no one liked their friendship and many didn't understand it, but they were bonded and they wanted it to be for life.

One Year Later
Annie's parent's biggest fear had become a reality. Their daughter had become a major problem. She was constantly suspended from school because she fought

often, and she skipped classes just as frequently. She had even gone as far as to curse out one of her teachers. She was not liked by the students in school. Her only friend was Doc and that was just fine by her.

Doc trusted Annie. He understood her and didn't mind that she was rough around the edges. She was honest and he knew he could rely on her. Annie too knew about Doc and she didn't judge him. He truly loved Annie and when he confessed his deepest sins to her, she didn't change or get distant. She simply promised not to tell anyone about the murders he committed and Doc felt a since of relief that he was finally able to tell someone about his deadly secrets.

Annie had secrets as well. Though they may not have been as dark as Doc's, she too had skeletons in her closet. Annie was a very outgoing girl. So much so that she was sexually active and had, had two abortions. The man she was sleeping with was twice her age and he kept their sexual relationship going by following her to Lancaster. Her male suitor lusted young Annie so deeply that being caught was not his biggest fear; but the idea of not seeing, touching, and tasting the young girl was his only concern. Annie was out of control and her parents could not help her. They were stuck in a world of denial because they still were under the impression that Annie was a virgin.

Annie was spiraling out of control and no one could help her. Doc was a bit concerned about her but kept his focus on his schooling. He knew he was going to college after being skipped twice and now sixteen and a senior in high school, not even his love for his friend could take him off track. He was slated to attend Harvard in the fall.

Chapter 13
September, 1977

Marabella and Annie's mother, Joan, watched as Doc and Annie got inside of her father's station wagon. Annie's father, Tony, was kind of enough to offer to take Doc to his new home-Harvard University. Doc had received a full scholarship to the prestige university which was located in Cambridge Massachusetts, and he was eager to be rid of the small town of Lancaster. He wanted his freedom and to be around like minded individuals. He needed knowledge. It fueled him and he knew attending Harvard he'd be up to his knees in what he loved most.

Marabella walked up to the car and gave her son a kiss on the cheek. She had watched her son suffer enough heartache and today was a day of pride, hope, and new beginnings. After a brief farewell he focused on the path ahead of him and the trio pulled off.

During the long trip Annie and Doc discussed his future and their friendship. They made a promise to stay in touch as much as they could and to never forget the bond they shared. It was a tough ride because as they got closer to Doc's new home, the reality of their six hour separation began to sink in. Neither of them knew the next time they'd be able to see each other but they both hoped that it would be sooner than later.

Once on campus a student directed them to the Longwood Medical Building. Doc would be staying inside of the adjoining building; which housed many of the freshman dormitories. After unloading his things, Doc walked back towards the vehicle with Annie. His life had now changed. He was only sixteen years of age but about to embark on a very mature mission. He wanted his friend's support and had wished the cards she were dealt

could have landed her in the dorm next to him; but he knew they were walking on two extremely diverse paths.

"Best friends forever," Annie said, as she hugged Doc closely and her tears fell onto his shoulders. "Best friends for life," he said, as he struggled to hold back his tears. "Remember to call me on the weekends and stay focused on your studies," Annie said, as she tried to gain her composure and walked over towards her father.

Doc smiled at his friend and thanked her father once again for the ride. He was nervous but had to sink the butterflies in his stomach and face his fears. He wanted this. This was his destiny. He would become a doctor.

Chapter 14
A Few Months Later

College was not that different than high school when it came to Doc having friends; he didn't have any. He was not popular, nor was he on the road to being cast as the leading man on campus. He was back to being a loner and excelling in his studies. His professors saw him as an intellect and many of them enjoyed watching him learn at ease. It was as if he had a photographic memory and they were in awe at how much he knew, and at how much knowledge he could consume.

Doc was focused but he did have a pressing issue that was troubling him on campus. Simon Conners, a rich and cocky kid from Austin Texas had made his way to Harvard. Many who knew that it's not always about what you know, but who you know, would tell the truth that Simon's oil typhoon father was the only way he had made it into the prestigious school of Harvard University. His father knew politicians and people in high places; and he had greased many palms to ensure his family had the best of the best.

Simon was a good-looking, slim, Caucasian male. He was liked by many and anything he wanted, his father made sure he had it. He drove a red Porsche and wore the latest and trendy clothes and shoes. He was privileged and living the silver spoon life. Doc was stuck with him for a roommate.

When Doc tried to study at night, Simon would become agitated and turned his radio up as loud as it would go to disturb Doc. He was a horrible roommate and had no consideration. When he snuck females into their room he never asked if it would be okay because Simon did what he wanted to do when he wanted to do it. Clearly

it was not a good connection to pair the two opposites in the same room.

Doc despised the rich southern brat and he was not afraid of Simon. He wanted to have a good college experience but the eighteen year old freshman was making that idea impossible. Doc had no respect for him. He looked at his roommate as someone who had never earned a dime and had the world handed to him. Doc knew it would be only a matter of time before the blue eyed young man would push him over the edge; but with all his might he was trying to control his rage. Doc had a thing for blue eyes. They were the tastiest and if Simon didn't straighten up and get in line Doc may have a treat sooner than he had expected.

Chapter 15
December, 1978
Three Weeks Prior To Christmas Break

Doc's fingers were on overdrive as he typed away on his typewriter. The sound of the flushing toilet didn't slow him down as his roommate Simon walked out of the bathroom and confronted him.

"City Slicker I'm gonna need you to keep all that noise down. I'm having some company tonight and maybe you can find something to do besides make noise," Simon suggested, as he took a sip of his cold Coca Cola. "I have an important exam in the morning," Doc said harshly. "Well then when I get back in just keep it down and stay out of the way," Simon ordered. "Don't worry cowboy, I'll just put up the blanket again so you can have your privacy," Doc said, as he continued to type his paper. "Well good. I'm bringing two pretty little bunnies over tonight and if you're a good lad I just might let you have a piece of one," Simon said with his southern accent. "Really," Doc said, as a smile grew upon his face. "Just calm your hot tail down boy. First let's see how tonight plays out. You can't be making all that noise and you've gotta let loose a little. You're too uptight and I can't have you scaring my honey bunnies away," Simon said.

Doc stood up from the chair and looked at Simon and asked, "How can you have sex with so many women? Don't you get tired," Simon smiled at Doc and said, "Women are like this Cola in my hand; no matter how many sips I've had, I always want another."

He took his Cola and drunk all the contents before slamming the empty bottle onto Doc's desk. "Take care of that for me Doc. I'll be back in a few hours," Simon said as he walked out of their room.

Lancaster, PA

Annie was inside of her bedroom smoking marijuana and watching television. Since Doc left for college she had not been the same. Her attendance at school dropped and her drug habit had gotten more of her attention. She had become hard to deal with and each day she argued with her parents. Annie felt alone and she didn't know how much Doc's absence would affect her, but she could tell that she was truly missing her friend.

Talking to him on the phone just once a week was not enough to fill the void that grew inside of her heart, and to fill that gap she found other ways to occupy her time. Sex had become another hobby of hers that got a lot more attention, and she now explored it with a few of the local boys in her town; and some not so young boys as well. Drugs and sex was her thing and she wanted more of what a big city could offer. She was bored to death with Lancaster, Pennsylvania.

Annie wanted to get back to Philadelphia. She wanted to be back with her friends and family, but her parents needed to stay in Lancaster for her father's job; and they enjoyed the calmness of the country. The more they tried to push the idea of her settling down in their new town, the more Annie rebelled and begged to be taken back to her old West Philadelphia neighborhood.

As Annie sat on the edge of her bed she heard the approaching footsteps of her father. She didn't care if he knew she was smoking because she was tired of hiding her lifestyle. She had reached her boiling point with her parents and could care less about the consequences they would place upon her.

"What the hell do you think you're doing," her father Tony yelled. "Just leave me alone," Annie shouted. Tony walked over to Annie and grabbed her shirt. "Don't

you ever talk to me like that again," he screamed. His eyes were stern and the grip he had on his daughter was a clear indication that he had enough of her crap.

"Ever since we moved out here you've been acting up! I'm trying to give you a better life and you're fighting me every chance you get. I'm sorry you don't have friends here and I'm sorry Doc left, but if you get your shit together you'd be moving on to better places as well! You're messing up your life and I don't want you to destroy yourself but I'll be damned if I let you run all over me in my house!"

Tears rushed down Annie's face as her father continued to scorn her. She knew he was telling her the truth and that her parents did care for her.

"Now open up the damn window and get that smoke out of here," her father demanded. Annie's mother was standing in the doorway of her daughter's room. Her face was filled with disappointment and she was overcome with sadness. Annie was hurt because she knew she was inflicting pain on her parents but she knew that she was not going to change. She wanted what she wanted and the only way she could get the life she yearned for was to leave her parents and the town of Lancaster. In that moment she had decided that she would move on.

Chapter 16
Freshman Dormitory
Harvard University

Doc was still studying and doing classwork as Simon walked into their room with two beautiful women; one smoking hot blonde and one full breasted brunette.

"This is my roommate," Simon said, as he walked past Doc with his arms wrapped around both ladies. Doc could tell from their bubbly nature that they had all been drinking.

Doc stood up and hung up the large blanket onto the self-made room divider. Although he could no longer see the action he could clearly hear everything that was happening on the other side of the blanket.

"Get undressed ladies and let's party," Simon shouted to his guest. Doc instantly became erect. Each time Simon would bring a female friend over and have sex with them, Doc would listen as the lust filled his body until he could no longer hold it in. Then he'd silently masturbate as Simon had his way with the ladies. This was the closest Doc had ever been to actually having sex. He had masturbated to photos but he had never been with a woman.

Hearing Simon approach the blanket Doc quickly stopped stroking himself. Simon pulled the blanket back and said to Doc, who was now sitting upright on his bed, "Come join us." Doc couldn't believe it but he was surely going to take his roommate up on the invite. "So which one can I have," Doc asked. "The brunette with the blue eyes. I think she digs you," Simon said.

Why was Simon being nice, Doc thought? It was not like him to share any of his ladies and this made Doc a bit skeptical. Simon was an arrogant, egotistical, selfish asshole and now he wanted to offer Doc something he had

craved for such a long time. Doc wanted to join in but he couldn't figure out why Simon would share. Doc's hormones began to rage within him and his logics were being knocked down. He started to tell himself that Simon was a cool guy, that they had to get to know each other better, and that everything would be fine. Doc didn't want to be a virgin anymore and his desire to end his virginity overrode any of his apprehensions.

"So are you joining us or not," Simon rushed. "Yes, I'm in," Doc excitingly said. "Good. Well get undressed and then come on the other side with us. Nothing but heaven on my side my friend, so take it all off and come on over," Simon said, as he walked back over to the ladies.

As Doc undressed he could not stop thinking about the beautiful blue eyed brunette. He had the urge to lick all over her and wanted to finally know what it was like to be inside of the warmness of a woman. He was eager and he was ready. He could hear the girls giggling and the sounds of kissing. This was the night he would lose his virginity.

Doc was undressed. He was nervous and sweat poured from his face and his palms were sweaty. His heart beat raced but it was now or never. He took a deep breath and swiftly pulled the thick blanket down. Once the blanket hit the ground Doc was standing nude as the flash of a camera went off.

He had been setup. The trio all had Polaroid cameras in their hands and they were fully dressed. They started to snap photos of Doc as he stood there in shock, with a hard-on. He was humiliated and knew he should have trusted his gut. Simon was an asshole that had never done anything nice for Doc and now he had shown exactly who he was.

Then to make matters worse these women were not random classmates. They both worked for the school's

paper. Simon had convinced the two ladies to help them pull of this prank and to have it printed in the school's newspaper.

Doc gave Simon a stare that could rip the heart of a lion out and then he slowly walked into the bathroom. He was fuming. He paced the small bathroom as his blood boiled. The laughter from the trio only made matters worse and he knew that he'd have to get his revenge. He would not forgive Simon for this prank and as he paced the floor he began to plot his revenge.

Suddenly he noticed two empty Coca Cola bottles in the trashcan. Simon would drink five to six bottles of the soda daily and Doc knew what he had to do. Simon's favorite drink would prove to be a weakness that Doc needed to get his roommate back.

Once Simon and the ladies left the room, Doc exited the bathroom. He put his clothes back on and thought about the moment he would get the Texan back. Simon had made a fool out of Doc and there would be consequences for his actions.

Moments later Simon walked back into the room. "No hard feelings City Slicker. It was all in fun," he said, as he laughed and sipped on his Coca Cola. "No hard feelings at all. I can take a good joke. You got me good," Doc said, with an evil grin on his face. "Enjoy your night," he said, as he went back to his studies.

Chapter 17

Early the next morning Doc's nude pictures were plastered all over the freshman dormitories. Wherever Doc went everyone was pointing, whispering, and laughing at him. He was a hot topic and another victim of the school's traditional freshman prank; but for Doc it was so much more. The humiliation ate at him and Simon had crossed the line. He would pay for what he thought was just a joke and while Doc sat inside of his class' laboratory he began to formulate his plan.

Philadelphia, PA

On the corner of 9th and Filbert Streets, with her black suitcase in hand, Annie stepped off of the Greyhound bus. Fed up with Lancaster and her parents desire to stay there, she ran back to the city she loved. She didn't know what the city had in store for her but with only thirty dollars in her pocket she was not turning back. Annie would rather face the unexpected in the streets of Philadelphia than to run back to the comforts of Lancaster.

Annie knew she had to avoid the familiar parts of the city where her family stayed. She knew her father had called her relatives and would come and try to force her back home with him. She didn't know where to go but she saw a potential lead.

Parked on the corner was a new, slick, black Cadillac Seville, and there were two handsome men standing beside it. Annie noticed one of the men counting a large sum of money, and then he passed it to the taller, darker, gentleman. In that moment the taller man noticed Annie. The man who had handed off the money walked across the street and got inside of his car and pulled off.

"Hey pretty lady. How are you," The man asked as he stood by his car. She walked closer to him and said, "I'm fine. I just got into town." He smiled and said, "That's nice. Well my name is Sonny. What's yours?" The young girl smiled and said, "My name is Annie." He got a feeling about the girl and felt he knew what he needed to say to play the game with this young and unsuspecting girl.

"Do you need a ride," he asked, as he grabbed her suitcase and placed it into the backseat. "Yes," she said as she entered his car. "How old are you Annie," he asked. "I'm sixteen but I'll be seventeen in two months," she said proudly. "Oh really. That's cool. I'm twenty-two," Sonny lied.

Annie looked at Sonny and she knew he was lying as they drove off. However, she didn't care how old he was because she had been with older men before and she was in need of being with someone that could help her out. As long as he had an apartment, his age didn't matter to her. She needed a place to stay.

Truth was, Sonny was thirty years old and a well-known pimp. He was downtown to collect his money and he often hung around the bus station searching for young runaways to add to his collection of prostitutes. Today was his lucky day. He had already scanned the young girl's body and had imagined the many ways he'd have his way with her. She was young and tender just like he enjoyed them.

Within twenty minutes they were inside of a motel in South Philadelphia. Sonny didn't hesitate. When the room door was closed he struck Annie and beat her hard. He threw her to the floor and sat on top of her as he ripped her clothes off. He placed his hand around her neck and began to choke her until she cried. Then he turned her over and fucked her like a dog that had been in heat for years.

Chapter 18
A Few Days Later

Simon was struck with a strange and unknown illness. He had uncontrollable vomiting, a high fever, and diarrhea. For three days he had been bedridden with serve pain and at times he was delusional.

"Are you feeling any better," Doc asked, as he took a seat next to Simon's bed. Simon could barely speak and his eyes were as red as apples. He was sweating and his forehead was on fire. "Here I brought you another Coca Cola," Doc said, as he passed his friend his beloved drink.

Simon was weak but managed to hold the bottle. He had drunk down the drink hoping that it would cool his body off. When he had finished the soda, Doc smiled and discarded the bottle. He had to get back to class so he asked his roommate, "Is there anything you need before I go?" Simon was tired and softly replied, "Just get out of here so I can sleep."

A Few Hours Later

Doc had a long day. One of his classes flooded him with exams and he just wanted to get back to his room so he could rest. When he got to his dorm he noticed a small crowd of onlookers and an ambulance parked in front of the entrance. Then he watched as the paramedics brought Simon's lifeless body out on a stretcher. Everyone was shocked and many of the students gathered were crying. Doc stood emotionless as they loaded him into the back of the ambulance and then he walked to his room.

Doc sat onto his bed and started to laugh. Simon Conners had gotten exactly what he deserved and Doc was delighted that he was dead. He knew that he'd never let the embarrassment he suffered at the hands of Simon fade

away. So, when he secretly stole liquid Polonium he knew just how he would use the deadly poison. The liquid form of Polonium is a radioactive poison, a sure killer and has no known cure. It is also very hard to detect in the human body so it was Doc's first choice.

Each Coca Cola that Simon enjoyed had been tainted and because the poison gave off no taste, Simon drank his beloved soda without any suspensions. For four days, Doc put a moderate dose in each bottle of soda he found, and it didn't take long for the poison to attack Simon's body and shut down each and every one of his vital organs.

"Now I can study in peace," Doc said, as he lay back on his bed before falling into a deep sleep.

A Week Later

The doctors at the nearby hospital determined that Simon had died of an apparent heart attack. There was evidence that he had a heart murmur and an abnormal heartbeat; and since they could not figure out exactly what was causing his symptoms and organ failure they settled on what they could prove. No traces of Polonium were discovered in his system, his death certificate was signed, and his father was left to plan his son's funeral.

In the meantime Doc had now gotten a new roommate. His new roomy was a Chinese exchange student named Lee Chang. He was a quiet nineteen year old that could barely speak a word of English and he stayed himself.

Christmas Break

After arriving in his hometown of Lancaster, Doc was excited to see his mother and Annie. When he stepped off the bus he walked down the road to his home. Once inside of his house his mother was standing in the living room with tears in her eyes. She had missed her son madly and was excited to see him. Doc hugged his mother and kissed her softly on the check. He loved her.

Doc never bothered asking about his stepfather or even going up the stairs to see him. No matter how much time passed, or where he went in life, he'd never forgive the man who tortured him with sexual and emotional abuse when he was a young boy.

His mother had a warm, home cooked meal waiting for him and he enjoyed every bite. It took Doc no time to finish his meal and as soon as he was done he headed next door to see his best friend. He missed her and was wondering why she hadn't called him in a while. When Doc knocked on the door, Annie's father answered it.

"Hey Doc, how are you," Tony said. "Hello Sir, I'm doing well. Is Annie home," Doc said excitedly. Annie's father facial expression changed dramatically and he said, "I'm sorry but she ran away a week ago. She went back to Philadelphia but I haven't been able to find her yet."

Hearing that his best friend had ran away hit him hard. Annie was supposed to be home when he arrived and he had so much to share with her. They had to get caught up and he wanted to hear about the new things she had gotten herself into, but his friend was gone. He didn't know why but his intuition told him that she was in a great deal of trouble.

Chapter 19
Early The Next Morning

Doc watched as his mother fed his bedridden stepfather a bowl of warm oatmeal. She had no idea that Doc had placed a large dose of Polonium inside of his meal. Doc was fed up with his mother caring for John. He saw no reason for him to continue living because he was never going to get better. The man he hated was draining his mother and he wanted to put him out of his misery.

Early the next morning Doc was awakened to a knock on his bedroom door. His mother's face was somber and she looked pale.

"John is dead. His body is so cold and he's not breathing," she said as tears fell from her eyes. "Okay. Just let me know when the funeral is. I am here for you but I don't care about the dead mother," Doc said, as he closed his eyes and went back to sleep.

Philadelphia, PA

Sonny had Annie's naked body bent over the bed as they faced a huge wall mirror. Fucking his young new whore in the ass was a part of his daily routine. Sonny was Annie's pimp and any way he wanted her, he had her. She didn't put up a fight and gave in to all his demands. Annie had become a real life puppet and Sonny pulled all the strings.

Annie had become Sonny's number one recruiter and he sent her out often to bring in a new batch of fresh faces. He wanted them young and he loved runaways. He knew that many of them were screwed up emotionally and he could bend them until he broke them; and then he'd control them. So far she had fetched him a young girl

named Gia, and her reward was another hard fuck in the ass.

After Sonny finished sodomizing Annie, he reached under the bed and took out a small brown leather bag. The bag held the contents of a few syringes and a couple bags of heroin.

"Daddy please don't make me use that," Annie begged. "Shut up bitch and do as I say. You're not a little girl anymore you're a full-fledged whore and this is what all my hoes do," Sonny instructed.

Annie did not utter another word because she knew the consequences if she had talked back to her Daddy. She stood still as he tied a small rubber string tightly around her arm and stuck one of the syringes into her virgin veins on her left arm. Sonny smiled as he watched his young whore slip into a world of darkness. He knew the smack that he stuck in her arms would have her hooked forever.

Sonny laid Annie's limp body onto the bed and then he tied himself off and injected the liquid fusion into his arm. He was now riding a cloud that took him to a euphoric place as he lay back on the bed and drifted higher.

Chapter 20
Three Days Later

Doc had decided to postpone his return to school. His stepfather was dead and he needed to support his mother at the funeral. John had died of cardiac arrest and thanks to Doc's new friend, Polonium; no one would know the true cause behind his stepfather's demise.

Doc and his mother Marabella stood by John's grave as they listened to the Pastor reading a few versus from The Holy Bible. The ceremony was small, with only a few of John's former coworkers in attendance. Neither Doc nor his mother showed emotion as the funeral ended. A burden had been lifted off of Marabella's back and she was relived; and Doc was just elated to know the monster he knew as his stepfather was dead.

When Doc and his mother returned home they had a peaceful dinner and watched television together. His mother had clearly grown tired and she told her son, "I'm heading up. I'm exhausted. I know you need some rest since you have to get up early and get back to school, so don't stay up too late." Doc kissed his mother on the check and watched as she walked up the stairs.

After his mother had fallen asleep, Doc grabbed a shovel and left the house. He walked down a dark street that led to the old cemetery. As soon as Doc reached John's freshly covered grave he began to dig. He dug nonstop for about an hour until his shovel banged into his coffin. Once he had it opened he reached inside of his backpack and removed the long meat clever.

Without hesitation he began to use the sharp blade to remove the head of his stepfather. He then placed it inside of a black plastic bag before he closed the casket and began to rebury his stepfather.

When he was finished he returned home and cleaned himself off. He hid his stepfather's head in his closet. He was sure to double bag the head as he placed scented oil in his closet to ensure the smell of rotting flesh was sealed within the bags. He knew he wouldn't have to hide the smell too long because the next day when he returned to school he would dismantle the head and feed it to the lab rats he tended to.

Chapter 21
February 1980
A Year Later

Doc sat on his bed as he watched the U.S. Olympic hockey team defeat the Mighty Russians. He wasn't a big sports fan but it seemed like everyone on campus had caught the Olympic bug. After the game ended Doc took out one of his XXX-rated video cassettes and placed it inside of his VCR. His roommate, Lee Chang, was in the library studying so Doc had some time to himself. He pressed play and sat back as the action began.

Masturbation was normal for Doc. This eighteen year old virgin was filled with hormones that often left him feeling unsatisfied and thirsting for more. He wanted to experience the real deal and lately having sex often filled his mind more than his studies. He was becoming obsessed with the idea of having intercourse and there were moments where he had thoughts of sleeping with men and animals; which all seemed perfectly normal to him.

Doc wanted to find a prospect to free him from his virginity but too many females found him creepy; and pretty much everyone else shared their sentiments. Many nights he'd walk the campus scouting possible candidates but his quest was not rewarded.

Filled with lust but unable to relive himself with another being, he continued to thrive in school. He was one of the top medical students on his campus and one of his professors told him that he'd graduate Summa-cum-laude if he continued on his pathway of success. Doc was destined to become a medical doctor and tried to keep his focus as he struggled with his sexual desires.

Six months later in August, Doc landed a job in the school's morgue. The school had cadavers which they used to help with research and to teach medical students about the human body. Doc loved being around dead bodies and this job suited him well. He showed up early for his shift and often stayed later than required. He never missed a day and felt at peace being in that quiet, cold, stiff atmosphere.

Doc's mind was full but he still had space in it to think about his best friend Annie. She hadn't called him in over a year and he worried about her. He tried calling her parents but they too had lost contact with her. He didn't know if Annie was dead or alive. He felt as if somehow he had abandoned her but he had to press forward with is calling for medicine.

While sitting in his classroom his professor began to speak proudly. "Harvard graduates invented the iron lung, cultivated the Polio virus that led to vaccines, introduced insulin to the United States, mapped the visual system of the brain, created the external cardiac pacemaker, and even developed artificial skin as well as conducting the first ever successful kidney transplant and so much more. To be a student at Harvard is a privilege and distinguished honor. When you graduate you will be equipped to help design innovative solutions for complex medical treatments, cures, and clinical strategies and technologies."

Doc was tuned into every word. To be a part of a university that had produced so many great minds made him feel proud and special. As he continued to listen to his professor the class was interrupted by the school's PA system. "Randy Patterson please report to the main office." Doc was confused. Why had he been called? His professor excused him from class and Doc made his way to the main office.

"Yes, is everything okay," Doc asked the school's secretary. "You have an urgent phone call," she said as he handed him the phone. "Yes, this is Randy. Who's this," Doc asked. "Hello Randy I'm Doctor Stanley Klein and I am your mother's personal physician. I'm calling because unfortunately your mother is not well. It would be in your best interest to get home as quickly as possible. We don't have much time left."

Doc dropped the phone and ran out of the office. Nothing in this world would stop him from being with his beloved mother in her time of need; not even time.

Chapter 22
Three Days Later

Harvard had granted Doc an emergency leave to be by his sick mother's side. Marabella was dying from a severe form of brain cancer. Time was not on her side and it was certain that she would die sooner than later. For the past year she had been receiving treatment but she never told Doc. She didn't want to worry her son and have his mind taken off of his studies.

Doc sat beside his mother as he stared at her beautiful blue eyes. Her head had been shaved bald and the disease had eaten away at her body. She was thin, gaunt, and a former shell of herself. She could barely eat and had no desire to. She was often thirsty but didn't have the energy to drink so she had to have a constant IV in her arm to keep her from becoming dehydrated.

"I love you Randy," Marabella said softly. "Promise me that you're going to make me proud and become a famous doctor one day," she said. "I promise mother," Doc said, as tears fell from his eyes onto his mother's bed. "I promise I'll make you proud," he said. "Thank you son...thank you."

Doc watched as his mother became still and quiet. Her breathing calmed and became silent as she took her last breath. He rubbed his sweet mother's hands and tried to gather what was happening in front of his eyes. He felt his mother's pulse and he knew it was a reality. Cancer had taken his mother from him.

His pain turned to anger in an instant. Why hadn't doctors created a cure for cancer? Why couldn't these intelligent beings save his mother? Why had the one woman he loved been taken from him?

Alone in the house with his mother, Doc stood up and stared at her. He slowly began to undress Marabella

and then he removed all of his clothes. He cuddled up next to his mother as he told her how much he loved her. She was soft and enjoyed touching her flesh. Doc kissed her lips and said, "I love you. Thank you for giving me this moment."

Doc slowly slid his erect penis into his mother's corpse and began to penetrate her. This was the first time he had ever been inside of a woman and it was everything he had imagined. The fact that he was able to lose his virginity to his mother made the experience even more memorable.

It didn't take Doc long to explode inside of his recently deceased mother. He couldn't get enough of her and he continued to penetrate his mother's corpse. He knew this was a feeling that he'd never get enough of and the thought of returning to his school's morgue made him smile.

Chapter 23
A Month Later

Doc lay across his bed and he felt alone. His mother had died and his best friend Annie was gone. He wanted someone to talk to and he was struggling with the many demons that lived inside of him. The strangest thoughts constantly raced inside of his mind. Visions of death, murder and necrophilia acts all took up residency inside of his complex brain. Doc felt himself changing and he wasn't sure if it was for the better.

One day while sitting inside of the library, Doc sat down at the table reading. He was purging himself on news articles about serial killers. He read about Richard Trenton Chase, a killer that had been called "The Vampire of Sacramento," due to the fact he drank his victims' blood and had cannibalism tendencies. Right under that article was a story of Albert Fish; a man who had molested one hundred children. Then there was one on John Haigh, a serial killer from England during the 1940's who murdered six people and dissolved their bodies in sulfuric acid. Doc felt connected to all the men he read about. He understood something about them that no one could.

Since being molested as a child, Doc knew there had been a change inside of him that would never be adjusted or fixed. He hadn't felt normal and never thought it was possible to be like the people who surrounded him. He felt that counseling may answer some questions he had and he decided to schedule an appointment.

He put in a request to see Dr. Jane Trussell, a professor who was the head of the school's psychology department and the leading psychiatrist at his school. He had an urge to kill and a great desire to sleep with his new victim. The corpses at his school were not fulfilling his

needs and he needed a fresh kill. If she couldn't help him he'd have to kill again.

Chapter 24
Early Thursday Morning

Dr. Jane Trussell was a beautiful, mature single woman who was raising a teenage daughter. She was 5'9 and had long brown hair, with eyes as blue as the ocean. She was very respected within her university and in her field.

When Doc walked into her office she shook his hand and said, "Have a seat." She looked at Doc as he sat and said, "Mr. Patterson thank you for coming to see me. I want to ensure you that everything we discuss in my office will be held in extreme confidence." Doc said, "Okay," as she handed him a student confidentiality form for him to sign. She passed him a pen after he acknowledged reading the form and Doc signed the paper.

"So, how can I help you? What's on your mind," Dr. Trussell asked. After taking a moment Doc said, "I've been having a lot of weird dreams lately. I love your eyes…I've been having sexual dreams." Dr. Trussell ignored Doc's compliment about her eyes and said, "What type of dreams. Can you elaborate for me?"

Doc was becoming hypnotized by the Dr. Trussell's eyes. He could barely focus on what he wanted to talk about as he rambled on about wanting to torcher people and put his sexual partners into bondage. Dr. Trussell listened intently as she observed the young man's body language. When Doc finished speaking she asked, "Are you currently sexually active?"

Doc thought about the question before he answered and said, "Not at the moment. No I'm not doing anything to anyone at the moment." She continued by asking, "How often do you have these dreams and thoughts?" Doc quickly replied, "Every single day; sometimes four to five times or more. I'm masturbating

every night before bed but that's not controlling my sexual appetite." She looked at him and said, "Well what about the bondage and torcher? Where is that coming from?"

"Well I get turned on by dominating and applying pain to my partner. Chocking, biting, and anything else that deals with submission is my fetish." Dr. Trussell listened on as Doc continued to reveal his sexual preferences.

Dr. Trussell was surprised at how open Doc was with her. She felt that she could ask him anything and didn't want to mess up the flow of their conversation so she pressed on.

"I want to ask you a serious question Mr. Patterson. Have you ever been violent with a woman before?"
"Yes I have. A long time ago."
"Did you enjoy it?"
"Yes, I did. Afterwards I wanted to have sex with her."
"What about men...have you physically hurt any men?
"Yes I have."
"How did you feel afterwards with them?"
"The same. I wanted sex."

Dr. Trussell was silent as Doc continued to open up to her. She knew she was dealing with a strange and possibly dangerous individual. He had tendencies that could lead him to be a sexual predator and she was extremely concerned.

"What comes to your mind when you see a child?"
"Nothing! I'm not a damn pedophile," he lashed out.

She was delighted to hear that he was not interested in hurting children but he still had some very serious issues which caused her great concern. The doctor felt as

though Doc also needed medication because there was something way off inside of his brain.

"What's on your mind right now Randy?"

"I want to tie you down, strip off all of your clothes and fuck you while I choke you until you go limp…I'm so sorry."

"Don't be sorry. I asked the question and wanted you to answer it truthfully. I want you to open up to me so I can help you. This is a safe place and the more you release your inner thoughts we'll be able to eradicate your fears and find out the connection to some of your desires. How are you feeling now?"

"A lot better Dr. Trussell. You have some very beautiful eyes."

"Thank you. Let's see each other very soon. I want you to control your sexual desire as best as you can," Dr. Trussell said as she noticed the large bulge inside of Doc's pants.

"In the meantime I want you to read this self-help manual I published a few years back. I think it will do you some good. Okay?"

"Healing the Unconscionable Mind," Doc said reading the title aloud.

"Yes. I think it can help you make better conscious decisions and my ultimate hope is that it will help you eliminate the desires to hurt others. The manual offers mental exercises that you can use daily. So I hope you will give it a try."

"Okay. I'll read it."

"Great. It was a pleasure to meet you and we'll be in touch soon."

After shaking hands with the doctor, Doc left her office. She returned to her desk and began writing.

Randy Patterson is an eighteen year old white male. After a brief session with this client it is my professional opinion that he has a form of Antisocial Personality Disorder (ASPD). It is also apparent Mr. Patterson may have a form of sociopathic behavior. I believe the subject should continue weekly visits and should be prescribed medication if his desire to hurt people does not subside, along with his excessive sexual cravings. With proper treatment the client should be stable enough to maintain a healthy and productive life. If the client does not continue with treatment there is a strong possibility that the violence and sexual urges he has will take over his life and cause him and others grave harm. Subject should be closely monitored.

After closing her notepad, Dr. Trussell sat back in her chair and continued to think about her session with Randy. He had been the second man that she had diagnosed with sociopathic behavior. The first man was Charles Manson. She was granted a one on one interview with him in San Quentin State Prison. He was a serial killer serving a life sentence and the calmness in how he spoke reminded her of Randy Patterson. The similarities in the two made her make a mental note to have all of his professors keep an eye out on Randy. He was strange and if he did anything that would raise an eyebrow, she wanted to know. She knew she couldn't expose anything they spoke about to his professors but she wanted to do her best to keep everyone on campus safe; because in her mind she knew that Randy Patterson could end up being a really big problem.

Chapter 25
A Few Days Later

Lee Chang was sleeping soundly when he felt someone rubbing on his lower back. Quickly he jumped up to see his naked roommate Doc staring him down. Doc didn't say a word but he stared at Lee Chang as if he was waiting for his roommate to confront him. Since becoming roommates with Doc, Lee kept his distance. Doc was strange and Lee didn't understand his peculiar ways.

"What wrong Randy," Lee asked in his heavy accent. Doc didn't reply. He continued to look into his roommates eyes as lust filled his body. The smaller male was like a sirloin steak ready to be served on a platter. Doc had been planning his next move for over a year now. He knew his roommate would be returning to China in two days and if he was going to do it, now was the time.

In one swift move Doc overpowered his weak roommate and placed his hands into a pair of handcuffs. He pulled out a long hunting knife and placed it to Lee's neck and said, "Say one word and you'll never see China or your family again." Lee did as he was told and didn't utter a sound.

Doc began removing his roommates clothes and smelling his skin. He was turned on and couldn't wait to get a piece of the scared male. Doc took a black belt and wrapped it around his roommate's neck before laying Lee on his back and straddling him. Then he rammed his erect penis into Lee's virgin asshole. The deeper he stroke, the tighter he pulled the belt around Lee's neck. Lee struggled but did not cry out. Lee gave in and allowed Doc to have his way with him as Doc enjoyed every minute of it until he exploded deep inside of Lee's bottom.

Two days passed and as planed Lee Chang was back on a plane to his homeland. The humiliation he felt

had never left and he didn't understand why he had been Doc's target. Lee was not a gay man and had never given Doc any indication that he was interested in having sex with him; but the deed had been done.

As he started the long journey home he promised to keep the ordeal to himself. He would take the secret to his grave. His only mission now was to get as far away from The United States of America and Randy "Doc" Patterson as he could. He would never visit the country again.

Chapter 26
1982
Two Years Later

Doc did everything he could to keep a low profile after he had raped his roommate Lee Chang. Since Chang had returned to China, Doc had gone through six roommates. None stayed long enough to encounter the fate of Chang because the odd Doc was too much for them to stomach.

Doc still excelled in class and was seeing Dr. Trussell on a biweekly basis; but the sessions did nothing to control his impulses. The only reason he kept attending the sessions were to get another glimpse of her beautiful blue eyes. Each time he saw her he would return to his room and masturbate as he pictured himself choking her and licking her eyeballs.

Doc's obsessions kept him busy but he found time to think about Annie. He called her parents often but each time he did they still had not gotten word from her. It had been three years since he had heard his friend's voice and he longed to know how she was.

Thoughts of his future were also invading his mind. He promised himself that after he finished up his residency he'd move to Philadelphia and start his practice there. He was halfway through the eight year process and he knew he would succeed with his goals. He also wanted to be close to Annie. He was going to find her when he was finished with school. Also, Doc had gotten a nice amount of insurance money when his mother died so he didn't have to worry about the startup money for his practice. He had a plan and was going to stick to it.

But for now, Doc was focused on his desires that often overtook him. Inside of his dorm he secretly watched his female counterparts as they walked around campus. As

he looked through his binoculars he masturbated to the unknowing victims.

Doc was reaching his boiling point. Everything he did to keep from fulfilling his true desires was no longer giving him the gratification he needed. He wanted what he wanted. He wanted to taste Dr. Trussell. He wanted to do sadistic things to her without limits. He wanted to choke, spank, and abuse her before having his way with her sexually. He could feel his hands around her neck as he choked her until she passed out and he could not control his urges as he exploded all over his sheets.

Chapter 27
One Week Later

The winter sky was pitch-black and there were only a few stars that were visible by the naked eye. It was 10:45p.m. and Doc was ready to hash out his devious plot. Dr. Trussell had no clue that she was being watched through a pair of black binoculars. For almost an hour he had been waiting to get a glimpse of her.

Doc ducked down between parked cars as he clutched a seven inch blade in his right hand. Dr. Trussell stepped into the teachers' parking lot and calmly walked toward her car. This evening, she was alone and the only person in the parking lot besides Doc. Dr. Trussell got inside of her car and was quickly met by a masked man holding a long blade.

"Don't scream or try to get away or I'll kill you right here," her capturer said. She was terrified, and since she wanted to stay alive she obeyed his commands. "Please you don't have to do this! I have money you can have it," she pleaded. "Money is not what I'm after so shut your damn mouth," he said, as he threw her into the back of the car.

Dr. Trussell was petrified. She sat in the backseat unsure of why this was happening to her. She thought of her daughter and tears raced from her scared blue eyes.

Doc sat the knife down on the seat next to him as he began to pull his pants down. Dr. Trussell caught the mistake and knew she would have only one opportunity to escape from this crazed man. Instinct kicked in and Dr. Trussell began to kick the back of his chair and then she clawed at his face, kicking, punching, and doing anything she could to hurt the man. Doc was caught off guard and during the scuffle the knife had fallen to the floor.

Dr. Trussell saw him reaching for the weapon and immediately she reached for the door handle and exited the vehicle. She ran through the parking lot screaming for help as he made her way back towards her office.

Doc was fuming! He'd lost his prize. He grabbed his knife and quickly made his way from the car. He was angry at himself for not thinking his plan through fully. He had made a huge mistake that could cost him his freedom but more so he was frustrated that he was not able to have his way with the sweet blue-eyed doctor.

Chapter 28
The Following Day

The police's presence at Harvard University was felt as they did a full investigation into the attempted abduction and rape of Dr. Trussell. The press had picked up the story and they too were on campus. The school was known for many positive accolades and they wanted the crazed man caught quickly so things could return to normal.

Since the man was wearing a mask, Dr. Trussell was not able to give authorities much of a description. She didn't even recognize his voice as fear had dulled her senses and the fright from the experience had made the ordeal difficult to remember. Her only aim was to free herself from being raped and possibly murdered.

Following her assault, the school added extra security and installed new cameras in the parking lot; as well as placing cameras and lights in dimly lit areas around the school. If the masked lunatic planned on returning, the school was sure to capture him on camera this time so they could identify the crazed man.

Upset and frustrated, Doc sat in the back of his microbiology class. As his professor spoke to the class, Doc was lost in his own world. He didn't care what was being said because his mind was stuck on his prize that had gotten away. He had been sloppy and allowed his hunger to taste Dr. Trussell interfere with the techniques he should have used.

He wasn't concerned about the class because in his second year he had already passed the mandatory United States Medical Licensing Examination. He knew he was going to be a doctor and taking these classes were just protocol for him.

When class ended Doc skipped out on his Pathology class and returned to his room. He had gotten a new roommate, a young man named Julio, who was from New York. Being as though his roommate was in class, Doc went through his XXX-rated video collection and found something suitable to watch.

He had been fighting his urges all day and he needed to relieve himself. As the video played and he watched two women being pleasured by a horse, he began to enjoy himself as well. It didn't take him long to burst all over his hands and legs, as the thoughts of being with Dr. Trussell ran though his mind.

Chapter 29
Philadelphia, PA

On the corner of 43rd and Lancaster Streets, Sonny was sitting inside of his new Lincoln Town Car when he spotted a beautiful woman. She was waiting on the bus stop and she had a small child with her. He quickly spun his car around and parked his car near the female. He couldn't take his eyes off of her. She was stunning. Her smooth complexion and body of a goddess had him stuck.

Sonny got out of his car and approached the woman. As he walked closer she grabbed her son's hand as the stranger came near.

"Hey sweet thing. I ain't never seen you round these here parts before. What's your name," he asked. "My name is Pam and I'm not interested," she said bluntly. "But I ain't offer you nuttin yet baby," he said smoothly. "Well save it because whatever it is I ain't buying what you selling," she said. "Mommy who is this man," her son asked. "Nobody Norman," Pamela said.

Pamela was no fool. She knew exactly what business Sonny was in to and she wasn't about to be anyone's whore.

"I can change your life suga if you let me. You won't be standing on no bus stop if you let me take care of you," Sonny said, as he pulled out a large wad of cash. Pamela saw her bus coming down the street and said, "I'm fine. I don't need saving but you enjoy your day," she said as she walked onto the bus with her son.

Sonny got back into his car feeling the burn from the gorgeous woman's rejection. She would have made him plenty of money.

Moments later Annie appeared and walked over to his car.

"Here you go Daddy," she said, as she handed him some money. "Now can I get my fix," she begged. Sonny looked at her and shouted, "Bitch you better get the fuck out my face and go fuck some more tricks."

Annie walked away and made her way to find more clients. She had been working the streets since she was sixteen and now at twenty she felt burnt out. Heroin, cocaine, and Sonny's' constant physical and emotional abuse had taken a toll on her. Often she'd think about her parents and how they tried to save her, but there was nothing they could do now because she was caught up in the game. When she was sober the reality of her situation would send a stream of tears down her eyes and placed a burning sensation inside of her body; so she yearned to be high most of her day to numb her pain.

When she couldn't get high she had to think of the abuse her body suffered. She had been sexually active with so many people that once she reached five hundred, she stopped counting. She hated sex but she had no choice but to do what Daddy wanted her to do.

Annie had fought so hard to escape Lancaster and now that she was stuck in Philadelphia she had realized she made one of the worst decisions in her life. She had wanted to reach out to Doc but the humiliation she felt never allowed her fingers to dial his number. She knew he was doing well and she couldn't bring herself to tell him her truth.

As Annie walked down the street two tricks approached her. "How much for a threesome," one asked. "Three hundred up front and no condoms, no pussy," she said. "Okay, let's do this," they agreed.

Sonny watched closely as the trio made their way into one of his apartments. He knew the two tricks and they paid well for Annie's professional services.

Once inside they wasted no time having their way with Annie. They fucked her in every hole available and for an extra hundred dollars Annie allowed them to piss all over her face and body. It was all a part of the job and she was good at what she did; even though she hated every moment of it.

Afterwards she escorted the men from the apartment and went into the bathroom to clean off. She changed into some clean clothes and couldn't control the tears that raced from her face. She had fucked up her life and couldn't stomach this way of living anymore. With the four hundred dollars she had just made, she snuck out of the back entrance of the apartment. No longer could she endure this pain and even with a daily heroin habit, she knew she had to get away or she'd be stuck in this hell forever.

Chapter 30
April 1982
A Month Later

Doc was alone inside of the school's morgue as he sat at his desk filling out paperwork. He had just finished logging in a new female corpse that had been donated to the University by her family for the advancement of medical research. Doc couldn't wait to have her.

When he finished his work, he walked around the exam rooms and the office to the morgue to ensure he was alone with his new lady. Since his attempt to have Dr. Trussell was blundered for his sloppiness he had to be careful; not to mention security on campus had increased.

Working for Harvard's Medical Anatomical Gift Program proved to offer Doc a great reward because he was able to be around as many corpses as he wanted. Doc walked into the room where all the corpses were kept. Each was stored in horizontal refrigerators at a certain temperature to avoid decomposition. Doc walked over to the refrigerator that housed their new female cadaver. He picked up her cold, naked body and carried her over to a large exam table.

After dimming the lights and turning on the radio, he began to undress. This was a special occasion for him and he wanted to set the mood. Doc climbed on top of the table and cuddled next to the corpse as he spoke softly to her. He kissed and rubbed her body. The mood was perfect and then he began to penetrate her as he sucked on her stiff breast.

As he engaged in sexual activity with the female corpse the front door open. He was too far gone into his sexual escapade to hear the approaching footsteps; and the music was up a bit too loud.

Two campus guards had heard the music as they were making their rounds and decided to enter the morgue to ensure everything was fine. They called out twice to see if anyone was inside of the office and if everything was okay. Since they didn't get a response, they entered the room to see for themselves.

As they entered they could not believe their eyes. They didn't want to believe what they were seeing. They were disgusted and one of the officers could not resist the urge to vomit as the fluid spewed from his mouth. The other officer drew his weapon and instructed Doc to dismount the corpse and dress himself.

Doc was caught and he did as he was told. As he pulled up his pants and put his shoes back on, he knew he was in trouble but not sure what consequences he would suffer. He hadn't killed the woman. He had only enjoyed the internal openings of this lovely dead female.

He was handcuffed and led away.

Chapter 31
The Next Day

An emergency staff meeting was called to discuss and determine the consequences that Randy "Doc" Patterson had to face. Inside a large boardroom, Doc and five members of Harvard's staff were seated around a long oval table. The staff consisted of Dean Jules C. Bush, M.D., and the dean of medical education, Lee Gehrke PH.D.; who was also the associate director for the facility, Dr. Jane Trussell, Professor Richard Cartwright, and Dr. Samantha Fleming, a staff psychologist.

Doc was being charged "with sexual assault of multiple corpses", which was clearly a violation of the institutions regulations. After a thorough examination of their cadavers, they found traces of Doc's sperm in three other female corpses.

For over an hour the staff deliberated as they tried to determine Doc's fate. It had been a hard decision for them to arrive at because he was a talented and intelligent young man. There was no doubt that he'd be able to be a doctor but they could not afford to ignore what he had done.

The vote was in and it was four to one, Doc would be expelled from the prestige medical school and they placed a lifetime ban on Doc. He could never study at Harvard again. The only person to vote in his favor was Dr. Trussell. She had no idea that the man she was fighting for was her assailant and could have possibly killed her.

After hearing his fate, Doc sat at the table, motionless. He had ruined his life but he hoped that he could pick up and start somewhere else; but that would not happen. Dean Jules C. Bush was so incensed at the horrendous acts that he called over twenty-five

universities and shared the uncharacteristic acts of Doc with their enrollment staffers. Doc was blackballed and no university would accept him.

Security was called to escort Doc off the property. His belongings were already removed from his dorm room and the staff wanted him gone immediately. Dr. Trussell felt bad for the young man and before he departed she handed him a white card.

"What's this," he asked. "I made a call to a friend and this facility will help you. It's near your home state of Pennsylvania. I really think you will get the help you need here," Dr. Trussell said. "Why do you want to help me," Doc asked. "What you did was wrong Randy. It cost you so much but I still believe that inside of you there is someone special who will help so many people. Once you can control your urges and place that energy into your talents, you could leave a legacy that many generations will know of; but you have to get help."

Doc nodded his head as he read the card that said "Penn-Hurst Institution for the mentally and physically disabled." He was still skeptical of why she was helping him. "Do you really think this place will help me," Doc asked. "Yes I do. Director Winston is a wonderful psychologist and a graduate from Harvard. He's helped so many people who have been labeled helpless. If you want the help you can get it there," she said. "Okay I'll go there," Doc said. "Great. Go straight there. I already called and they will be waiting to help you. I'll call and check with you often to check on your progress," Dr. Trussell said.

As Doc waited along with the security guard for his cab to arrive, he thought of getting himself together so he could get back to his studies. Dr. Trussell and Dean Bush also waited on his ride. When the cab approached, security

helped put his belongings in the trunk and sent him away with the hopes of never seeing him again.

"Did he accept the offer," Dean Bush asked, as Doc pulled away in the cab. "Yes, he's on his way there now," Dr. Trussell said. "Good because that crazy son-of-a-bitch needs help immediately and Penn-Hurst will be the perfect place for him," Dean Bush barked. "Winston is waiting on him right now. He'll handle it," Dr. Trussell said. "What did he say," Dean Bush asked. "He said we have nothing to worry about and after a few shots of Benperidol he'll be a permanent resident," Dr. Trussell said. "Great because I never want to see that psychotic animal again. He has disgraced this university and now he'll pay for that. I don't trust him in any community and we just can't have the likes of Randy Patterson tarnish our reputation."

Chapter 32

As Doc was being driven away from campus in the back of the cab he had no clue about the conspiracy that had just taken place. The entire meeting he had sat in was planned and orchestrated. From the vote, to his dismissal from school, each person seated at the table played a role in this masterminded plan. Doc had thought he had a friend in Dr. Trussell but her vote to keep him at school was another part of the plot; her goal was simply to gain his trust and ensure his admission to Penn-Hurst.

Unbeknownst to Doc he was traveling to a mental facility that was dangerous, understaffed, and many State officials were lobbying to have the place shut down. They violated the constitutional rights of their patients and Dean Bush who knew of the faculties reputation had no qualms about sending Doc there, because he never wanted to see the man he called a walking lunatic again.

Once the cab pulled up to the small bus station which would take Doc on the next leg of his trip, he helped unload the young man's bags and drove off. Doc patiently waited for the bus to arrive as he sat in the practically empty station until he noticed an attractive young woman standing nearby. His eyes were immediately affixed upon her and he watched her every move. His sexual rage began to increase and his hormones began to boil over. He watched as she made her way to the bathroom. At that moment he felt for the knife in his pocket and got up and followed her.

Quiet as a mouse, Doc entered the bathroom and locked the door behind him. Quickly he located the stall with the woman inside of it and he made his move. He burst open the door and before she could yell out he grabbed her and slit her throat. Rage filled his eyes as he began to viciously stab the woman until he felt his erection

ready to burst out. Doc then pulled up her dress and began to have sex with the dying woman as he held her up by her neck.

The more blood that fell from her gave him a higher sensation, and he exploded his load of semen inside of her and pulled out immediately following the deposit. He rushed to wash as much blood off of him as possible as he changed into a pair of clothes that were in the backpack.

When he had cleaned himself, he calmly walked out of the bathroom to the awaiting bus. He quickly loaded his belongings and found his seat as the bus departed. Doc felt no remorse, only a sense of gratification that dwindled because the intended target was not his first choice. He longed to taste Dr. Trussell, and as he killed and had sex with the young woman in the terminal, the doctor was the only thing on his mind.

Chapter 33
Two Hours Later

Local authorities had the crime scene taped off and locked down. The brutal murder of this young woman was random and the type of crime that simply didn't happen. The victim had been stabbed over thirteen times and her throat was sliced from ear to ear.

As the detectives stood over the mangled female's corpse one shook his head and shouted, "This is the work of a goddamn savage!" His partner looked at him and said, "I hate to say this but we may have a serial killer on our hands. Our town does not need this shit," the officer said.

They began to process the scene when one of the detectives picked up the young ladies wallet and pulled out her identification. His face was shocked as he realized the nineteen year old victim was no stranger.

"You're not going to believe this," he said. "What is it Smitty," he asked. "This is Lisa Trussell. The daughter of Dr. Jane Trussell who works up at the University," Smitty said as he stared at his partner. "Fuck, I can't believe this," the detective yelled. "I'm going to get back to the station. I don't want to do this but we have to let Dr. Trussell know what happened to her daughter," Smitty said, as he walked out of the bus station's restroom.

Harvard University

The sounds of a grieving mother could be heard through the walls as Dr. Trussell screamed out in anguish. She had just received the heart wrenching news that her only child was brutally raped and murdered at a nearby bus station. Her daughter had been traveling to the school to pay her mother a surprise visit and no one could have imagined this would have been the outcome. The doctor

was in intense pain as she fell to the ground and wailed out. Her baby had been killed and as her fellow coworkers tried to console her, but they knew there was nothing that anyone of them could do for the grief-stricken mother. She was inconsolable and nothing could be said.

It had been just a few hours earlier that Dr. Trussell had sent a madman to the bus station where her daughter Lisa was waiting. Her plan to get Doc institutionalized had an unexpected snag in it and she had no idea that Doc was responsible for her daughter's death.

Chapter 34
Philadelphia, PA

"Did you find that runaway whore yet, "Hood asked Sonny. "No, not yet but when I do I'm gonna put my foot up her ass," Sonny said. Hood pitilessly stared at Sonny and said, "You need to control your whores. Maybe if you stop getting high you can focus on what the fuck is going on around you." Sonny brushed off the verbal lashing and said, "I'm cool man. I'm gonna find her soon because she can't be too far. I got this under control."

After Sonny paid Hood the thirty percent street tax he owed, they shook hands and Sonny got out of Hood's car. It had been over a month since he last saw Annie and each day that passed he was becoming more outraged at her disappearance. She might have been used-up but she was a whore that knew her stuff and made him a lot of money. The other girls he had on his roster could not bring in the money Annie did and he needed her back on his team; besides he had to make an example out of her. She was the first girl to leave Sonny and he didn't want the other girls to think they had that option. Not to mention other pimps had saw Annie's escape as a weakness in his rule and they were thinking about trying him. It wouldn't be too long before they would approach some of his girls and try to get them to work for them.

A few blocks away from where Sonny sat inside of his car, Annie was held up in a rundown motel. She lay in bed as she came down from her Heroin high. Even in her stupor she knew that Sonny was looking for her and wouldn't stop until she was back in his clutches. She was scared and thought Sonny might kill her if he ever found her, but she had to escape her pimp's abuse and the lifestyle he deemed the only way.

However, what Annie didn't understand was that Hood was a bigger threat to her. Any whore that messed with his money was a problem that he'd check if their owner didn't know how. Hood was the boss of the bosses. He ran the drug dealers and the pimps in his town. Annie kept a low profile. However, she still took risks when she hooked up with her faithful tricks and when she coped her drugs.

As Annie yawned and sat up on the bed, she felt the urge to use the bathroom. She made her way to the tiny washroom and cut on the lights. As the switched flicked, the lights on she caught a glimpse of herself in the mirror. Her reflection brought tears to her eyes as she saw the image of her reality. She looked beat down and the drugs had taken a toll on her body. She was not the beautiful, vibrant, youthful girl she once was. Annie stared in the mirror as she longed for the simple life when she would watch movies with Doc and argue with her parents; but she knew within herself those days were over and the opportunity to see her loved ones again might never present itself.

Chapter 35
Spring City, PA

Penn-Hurst Mental Hospital was originally known as the Eastern Pennsylvania State Institution for the Feeble Minded and Epileptic. Their doors opened in 1908 and housed some of the most unstable, sociopathic and psychic patients in the state. Lately, there had been so much controversy surrounding the institution and there were widespread talks about patient abuse that placed a black cloud over the facility.

When Doc arrived, he was immediately escorted to the director's office. Director Larry Winston had run the hospital for the past seven years. He was a Harvard graduate and held a master's degree in Psychology. He was a towering figure who stood at 6'5 and his imposing presence caused fear in his patients and in the staff that worked for him. Larry was a no nonsense type of guy and he ran the hospital like a boot camp rather than an institution for people with mental and physical disorders who needed help.

Before Doc's arrival, Dr. Trussell had spoken with Dr. Winston and faxed over all the notes she had kept on Doc. He assured her that he knew exactly how to treat his new patient and that she had nothing more to worry about. She was instructed by Dean Bush to destroy all of Doc's files, and he had compiled all evidence of Doc being a student and erased it from Harvard's memory. It was as if Randy "Doc" Patterson had never existed within their walls.

Dr. Winston watched Doc as he sat in silence. Doc observed the man who he thought favored a linebacker more than a psychiatrist and kept quiet. As Doc continued to observe the man who had been sitting at his desk reading his file, Dr. Winston began to speak. "Name,

Randy Patterson. Parents, both deceased, only sibling, deceased, age, twenty, height, 5'10, weight, 165 lbs., religion-none, hobbies, none, marital status is single, no children, and a former student of Harvard with an extremely high IQ," Dr. Winston said with a slight grin.

Standing beside Doc were two male staff members who wore white uniforms. When Mr. Winston finished speaking he stood up from his desk and approached Doc.

"Welcome to Penn-Hurst," he said, as he extended his hand to Doc. As they shook hands, Dr. Winston looked at his staff members and quickly blinked his eye. Instantly they grabbed Doc and struggled to restrain him. Dr. Winston made his way toward his desk. He retrieved a syringe and rushed over to Doc and plunged it into his neck.

It had all happened so quickly. Doc was caught off guard and within minutes he was carried down the long hallway. His life at Penn-Hurst had just begun.

Chapter 36
Three Weeks Later

Like a prisoner, Doc was locked away in a padded room and strapped into a straitjacket. He was fed three times a day and had no use of a television or a radio. The only thing that surrounded him was four white walls. When Doc would become restless the orderlies would give him an unknown medication which not only caused him to relax, but to hallucinate as well. At night he would lie on his bed and call out, "Marabella, Marabella!" He often thought his mother was in the room with him when he was alone.

Once a day, Dr. Winston would come by Doc's room to check on his new patient. He wanted to have complete control over his new resident and would allow Doc to spend another week in isolation before he would have a one on one consultation with him. Doc was now under the mercy of Dr. Winston and there was nothing he could do about it. He had no family and no friends. In less than a month, Doc had gone from being Harvard's top performing medical student, to a prisoner of Dr. Larry Winston at Penn-Hurst.

Though Doc was heavily medicated, he was able to understand that there was more to his story than he had been told. He knew if he ever wanted to see the outside of Penn-Hurst he had to be the best puppet to his puppet master. The more thought he gave to his entrapment, he knew that Dr. Trussell had to have had knowledge about the institution that she sent him to. It was all a set-up and he was catching wind of the scheme.

Penn-Hurst was a horrible place and at night the loud screams of the patients echoed through the hallways and bounced off the walls. It was like being stuck in a huge castle with living ghosts; who fought and killed

demons that never rested. Yet in the daytime there was a silence that crept out the soul. Most patients were heavily medicated during the day and staff members rarely ever spoke when they were in patients' quarters.

One day Doc sat on his bed and his mind raced as his plot for revenge began to brew. His placement in Penn-Hurst had been no accident and Dr. Trussell and Dr. Winston would soon pay for all the pain and torture he would undergo. It didn't matter to him how long it took to get his revenge because he knew one day he'd be free, and the people who set him up would enter their graves before schedule.

Chapter 37
1983
A Year Later

"How is Mr. Patterson doing," Dr. Trussell asked, as she spoke into her phone's receiver. "So far so good. The meds keep him stable and he's actually got a job helping out the orderlies with the other patients," Dr. Winston said proudly, feeling that he had made a major accomplishment because he had a sense of control over his patient. "Great. Does he still struggle with amnesia," Dr. Trussell asked. "Yes. This guy has no clue of who he is or where he comes from. He's lost and I own him," Dr. Winston said as he laughed.

"We call him Bob now," he continued. "Why Bob," Dr. Trussell asked confused. "We call him Bob because every day he watches The Price Is Right and stares at Bob Barker like he's his God. He doesn't say a word. It's hilarious but as long as he stays in line I'm fine with it," Dr. Winston said. "That's great because at the rate he was going he was destined to hurt someone. He could have even turned out to be a serial killer. Society is much safer now that he's away and I'm so glad I reached out to you," a thankful Dr. Trussell said. "Well he's not going anywhere and he won't be hurting anyone. Besides Bob loves it here," Dr. Winston chuckled. "But how are you holding up," he asked.

"I'm doing the best I can but it has been a tough year for me. Lisa's death is still unsolved and that doesn't help grant me closure; and they still haven't found a single suspect. Only a psychopath would have done that to my daughter," she said as her mood quickly turned gloomy. "Well at least you got one psychopath off the streets. Lord only knows what he would have been capable of doing if he was free to roam the streets," Dr. Winston said. "Yes,

you are right. That's why I couldn't allow him to leave here without a plan in place. His mind was consumed with sex and murder. Each session we had he never talked about anything normal; everything was always extreme and dark," Dr. Trussell said. "I've read his chart but where do you think it all stems from," Dr. Winston asked. "We talked in detail and in my professional opinion it would have been from his stepfather. The molestation and mental abuse took a toll on him. Then to lose his mother and his friend, Annie; that didn't help matters either. It's as if he lost all love for people and his attachment to society," she said.

"Yes, this Annie figure. Who is she? He's mentioned her a few times," Dr. Winston asked. "She might have been his girlfriend. He said she was his only friend but I think that he made her up. I never saw him contact her and there was no one else who did either. People like Randy Patterson don't have friends. Their anti-social behavior keeps them locked away from experiencing real love and with his appetite to torture and hurt people, today I have no doubt she's a figment of his imagination," Dr. Trussell said.

Chapter 38
A Few Days Later

Doc sat inside of his room as the orderly came by with his meal. "Here you go Bob. It's your favorite; chicken, mashed tatters, and corn. Oh and here's your mail too," Jessie said. "Thanks a lot," Doc said, as he sat back on his bed and opened his mail but was quickly interrupted. "Hey Bob, let me ask you something," Jessie said. "Yes. What is it," Doc said. "Why do you write all those companies," the orderly asked. "No real reason. Just something to do and they write back. I have no one else to talk to so it keeps me connected to the outside world," Doc said. "Okay. As long as Dr. Winston approves its fine by me," the orderly said as he left.

Doc opened up the large envelope he had been waiting on for over a week. The mail was from the Spring's city, City Hall Administration Building. As Doc pulled out the long folded piece of paper a smile came to his face. He held in his hand's Penn-Hurst's original blueprints and designs of the surrounding area. Doc knew when the placed was built and began to learn what he could about the institution that imprisoned him. He had a map in his mind of the entire city surrounding the hospital. Then he managed to steal a key from one of the orderlies that he worked with by taking it from the laundry while he washed their clothes.

It had been a year and each day he was planning his escape. Everyone thought Doc had forgotten who he was but no one could take his mind. He had them all fooled and his acting abilities were so solid that he had the great Dr. Larry Winston believing that he had trained and rehabilitated the beast inside of Doc. He had them all fooled.

After carefully studying the hospital's blueprints, Doc had learned where every exit was in the facility. He had already memorized the staff's schedule and daily patterns. He knew when they arrived, type of cars they drove, what they ate, if they were in a good mood and if things weren't good at home; he studied them like the astute student that he was. All he had to do now was wait for the opportunity to escape to present itself. There was no room for error and he had to get it right or face the possibility of spending the rest of his life at Penn-Hurst.

Chapter 39
Early The Next Morning

An orderly escorted Doc to see the hospital's physician and waited outside for the exam to end. All patients had to have at least one orderly with them while they traveled within the hospital. As Doc sat on the patient bed, all his vital signs were checked as Doc scanned the room. He had been making mental notes of all the equipment in the room since his first visit to see the physician.

Dr. Clifford Ford was an older Caucasian male in his mid-sixties. He wore thick spectacles and had very poor vision. Doc quickly noticed this weakness and saw that every few minutes the doctor would have to rub his eyes. The man who was supposed to be examining the patients was practically blind if he didn't have on glasses.

"You're in great health Mr. Patterson," the doctor said, as he put away his stethoscope. "What the hell is that," Doc stood up and shouted. "It's a rat," Doc said, looking around the office. "Are you sure," the doctor asked as he reached for his glasses.

This was his moment and he knew it. He knocked the glasses from the table and Dr. Ford stepped right on them. As he heard the glass break under his feet he knew he had just broken his spectacles.

"I need my glasses," The doctor said. "No problem. I'll go get the orderly to help you," Doc said. "Okay, please hurry up Randy."

During the entire time Dr. Ford was searching for his glasses, Doc had placed several medical items inside of his pocket. When the orderly arrived to help Dr. Ford get his secondary glasses from his car, he never thought to search their beloved and trusted Bob.

Once he escorted Doc to his room, the orderly went to Dr. Ford's car without any knowledge of the items inside of Doc's pants pockets. Doc sat on his bed and removed the medicine bottles and the syringes he had stolen. Then he securely tapped the items to the wall, which he hid by hanging up his large poster of Bob Barker back to the wall.

Chapter 40
A Few Months Later

As the screams of the tortured patients carried through the halls, Doc sat on his bed softly reading his notes. "Dr. Winston, Arrival time 9a.m., departure time-5pm, Car-grey Cadillac, office location-2nd floor, staff members on each floor-three, exit doors-left wing down back staircase, left hallway to parking lot, security-four, none in parking lot." Everything was set in motion and all he had to do was wait.

The next morning as he helped the orderlies clean up and mop the second floor. He was sure to stay close to Dr. Winston's office. He could hear the doctor speaking to a woman named Jane as he repeated the address of 724 North Concorde Road; which was in Cambridge Massachusetts. He also heard him agree to attend the party on a Saturday.

When the call ended Doc moved down the hallway as he continued to mop. Dr. Winston came out of his office and saw the orderly and his prized patient. "Hey Bob, you're putting too much damn water on that floor. It will take all day to dry so get some of that water up off the floor," Dr. Winston instructed. "Yes Dr. Winston," Doc replied, as the director of the facility walked away down the hall.

Later that evening Doc sat inside of his room looking at a map. He located the address on the map and it was the home of Dr. Jane Trussell; the woman who had tricked him into coming to Penn-Hurst hospital. She hadn't lived to far from the Harvard and he knew their next meeting would be sooner than she could ever imagine.

For now, just the thought of seeing his blue-eyed wonder sent sexual energy throughout his body. He

wanted to feel his hands around her neck as he choked the life out of her body. He craved the taste of her blood as he envisioned himself slowly slicing her flesh.

As Doc blocked out the loud screams of the patients, he mentally placed himself in a place where he could enjoy his night. As he pleasured himself in his room, filled with tranquility, he began to whisper, "Marabella," each time he stroked his penis. "Marabella, Marabella, Marabella," he said, until his erection came to a head and his sperm rushed from his penis and jumped all over his sheets.

Chapter 41
West Philadelphia, PA

"Bitch are you crazy! You didn't think I was gonna find you," Sonny said as he pinned Annie down to the floor. For the past forty-five minutes, Sonny had Annie trapped inside of her motel room as he beat her down. Thanks to Hood, Sonny had gotten word about Annie's whereabouts, and her pimp was able to locate her in the Blue Moon Motel.

"Bitch do you know how much money you cost me? Do you know how weak you made me look when your ass ran off," Sonny said, as he held a fistful of Annie's hair in his hand.

Without warning he pulled out his pistol and began to pistol-whip her. Her tears didn't slow him down as he continued to beat the girl until she fell out. She was unconscious and her face began to swell as the blood leaked from her head, eyes, nose, and mouth. Another one of Sonny's whores was standing by the door in total fear as she watched the brutal consequences they faced if they ran away from their pimp.

"Gia you stay here and clean this trifflin bitch up! Don't leave this room for nothing or your ass is next," he said, as he put his gun away and walked out of the room. Sonny placed a cigarette into his mouth and lit it. He thought to himself that he should have killed her. The only thing that stopped him was that she made him a lot of money.

As Sonny stood outside of the room, Hood pulled up inside of a new, black Cadillac. The window smoothly rolled down and Hood said, "Did you take care of business nigga?" Sonny grinned and said, "I sure did." Hood looked directly at Sonny and said, "Good because the streets were talking and it wasn't nothing nice. That

weakness you showed had them dudes ready to test you. People were questioning your abilities to Mack a bitch and I can't be down with no weak ass niggas. This game is about bringing in that money and having complete domination over all your bitches. You dig."

"Man, I'm cool. Let them talk. I got that bitch back and seven other bitches just like her; but trust me when I say she's learned her lesson. When she wakes up I'm gonna whoop that ass again just for fun, but that hoe know who her Daddy is," Sonny said, as he blew a cloud of grey cigarette smoke in the air, trying to play things cool.

"Yeah, that's what you need to do. Don't show no hoe no mercy and keep your shit in check. I don't play with none of my bitches and neither should you," Hood said, as he rolled up his window and drove off.

Sonny was left to think about what Hood had said. It was his final warning and Sonny knew if he didn't keep his whores in check the next pimp would be coming to collect them from him soon.

Chapter 42

Inside of the small, dimly lit female dormitory, Dr. Winston and one of his orderlies were strapping a female patient down to a bed.

"Hurry up and tranquilize her," Dr. Winston instructed the orderly. The staffer took out a long syringe and jabbed it into the female's neck. It would only take moments for the power narcotic to take control of her body and to leave her motionless on the bed.

"She got here a few days ago, Sir. Her name is Paula Ford, age twenty-five, and she has a diagnosis for bipolar and multiple personalities," the orderly said. "Okay. You can leave now," Dr. Winston said. "Yes, Sir. We have another female coming in later today and I'll be sure to come and get you as soon as she arrives," the orderly said, as he quickly left Dr. Winston alone in the room with the immobile female.

Once the room was cleared Dr. Winston began to undress the young woman. He knew that he had at least an hour with her before the medication in her system wore off. For years the doctor and his male staffers had been sexually assaulting the female patients they housed. Every time a new woman entered Penn-Hurst, Dr. Winston was first on the list to have his way with them. It had been seven years since he had taken control over the hospital, and for seven years he had raped and abused many of the female patients.

The abuse was not slated for the female population alone. Though the males were not sexually assaulted, they were beaten and verbally attacked. Nine months prior, nine members of the Penn-Hurst staff were indicted on charges that ranged from physical abuse to neglect of the elderly. The hospital was constantly criticized and there

were a few lawsuits pending against the organization; along with a petition requesting its permanent closure.

Dr. Winston didn't let any of those factors influence the way he did business. He continued to violate his oaths and ethical practices as he sexually assaulted and abused his patients, just like he was now doing. He laid his sweaty body on top of his newest female victim. He had no concerns about being interrupted, because outside of the door the head orderly guarded the entrance as he patiently waited for his turn.

Twenty minutes later Dr. Winston calmly walked from the room and gave his orderly a nod. The happy staffer smiled as he then entered the room and had his way with the unconscious female.

Chapter 43
January
1984
Seven Months Later

Doc sat down in his seat scanning the cafeteria while the patients ate their lunch. Nerves filled his body as the day's plans began to approach. All the key people and elements were in place, and after eighteen months locked away in the mental institution some called home. He was ready. He had been waiting for his moment and planning his escape. Today was the day he would free himself from Penn-Hurst.

As he looked on the wall he noticed the time was 12:18 in the afternoon. He stood up and walked over to Jessie; the orderly he had built the closest bond with.

"What is it Bob," Jessie asked. "I need to use the restroom. Those mashed potatoes did a number on me," Doc said, as Jessie laughed. "Okay, follow me."

They walked out of the crowded cafeteria and down a long hallway. As they approached the restroom Doc hurried inside and rushed to the last stall. He quickly stood on the toilet seat and pushed in the drop celling and removed a plastic bag he had placed there weeks earlier. Inside of the bag was a white staff uniform, a knife, and ten syringes filled with different psychotic medications that would paralyze the body.

Doc quickly changed into the uniform and placed all but one syringe into his pocket. After taking a quick breath he screamed loudly which caused Jessie to run into the lavatory. Jessie searched the stalls until he came upon the last one and he pulled the door open. Just then Doc lunged at him and stuck the syringe directly into Jessie's neck. There was a brief scuffle outside of the stall and

Jessie tried to put up a fight but the medication proved powerful as his body began to slump to the floor.

Doc dragged Jessie's body into the bathroom stall and closed the door. He then removed his hat and employee identification card and put those items on as he headed out of the bathroom.

Doc walked up the stairs and down the long hallway. The halls were empty because most of the staff and the patients were having their lunch in the cafeteria. He continued on his journey until he arrived at Dr. Winston's office. This was the time that the doctor took his daily afternoon nap and Doc thought it would be a great time to pay him a surprise visit.

Slowly, Doc turned the doorknob to his office and eased his way inside. Just as he predicted, Dr. Winston was asleep in his reclining chair and snoring as loudly as a grizzly. The sight of the doctor enraged Doc and his eyes quickly turned red with hate. He reached into his pocket and took out one of his syringes. Then he thrust the syringe into Winston's neck; which caused him to jump up. Doc strong-armed the man and held him in the chair as he covered his mouth. The medicine was fast acting and as Doc saw Dr. Winston losing his ability to speak he laid the man back down onto the chair.

Doc had a special treat for Dr. Winston. He removed the doctor's pants and then pulled out his knife. As he took a hold of the doctor's cock he looked at it and said, "This little thing is not worth having." He then began to severe the doctor's penis from his body.

Once it was removed he placed the blood soaked penis on Dr. Winston's desk. Then he rushed to the file cabinet and searched the drawer for his chart. The items were listed alphabetically and once he came across his name he pulled his chart out.

Grabbing a pen and a piece of paper from the doctor's desk, Doc wrote a note that read:

I am not ethically nor morally equipped to hold my position. I can no longer handle the stress and the responsibilities that come along with my duties. Furthermore I am truly sorry for the many females that I have raped and abused while in my care. I leave this piece of flesh with you all so that I can no longer hurt anyone in this world or another.

Dr. Winston

Doc then injected Dr. Winston with three more syringes which he felt would lead to his death. Afterwards he cleaned up any traces that would indicate that he was there and he tucked the folder into his pants, but not before taking Dr. Winston's car keys.

Calmly he walked down the hallway and when an employee noticed a few blood stains on his shirt, he didn't make a mention of it. They were so used to seeing the staff with patients' blood on their clothing that it became a regular sight in their positions.

As he entered the parking lot he didn't have time to enjoy the fresh air that sprung into his lungs. He rushed to locate the doctor's car and walked straight over to the vehicle. Upon entering the grey Cadillac he swiftly started up the car and began to pull off. One of the best things about being from a small town was that everyone in town knew how to drive and without that knowledge he would have been stuck; but thankfully for Doc it was a skill he had no problem executing as he drove away from Penn-Hurst.

The first part of his plan had been executed but as he rode away from Penn-Hurst he knew his taste of revenge had just gotten started.

Chapter 44
A Few Hours Later

When Dr. Winston's staff members noticed he had not made his normal rounds, one of his employees was sent to his office to check on him. Upon his arrival, he found the blood soaked body of the doctor, along with his severed penis. Dr. Winston was not dead and the distraught employee quickly called for police and for the staff's physician.

Soon after the body of Jessie was found in the bathroom; he had suffered a heart attack and died. His fellow employees tried to resuscitate him but there was nothing more they could do. Everyone became aware that Doc had escaped. A staffer searched the file cabinet to give what information or pictures of the patient they so lovingly called Bob to police; but they had nothing. It was a time when computers were not used and all files were hard copy, so the only people who knew of Doc and what he looked like were inside of that facility.

Other patients had escaped before and they were all returned, but Randy "Doc" Patterson was not about to be a return visitor to Penn-Hurst in this lifetime.

Later That Night
Cambridge, Massachusetts

Doc hid silently under the darkness of the night. He had located the address of the beautiful two-story home and waited patiently for his prey. The tranquil street was empty and perfect for the next stage of his plan.

As Dr. Trussell pulled her blue Ford into her driveway and parked her car, Doc's excitement grew. He had waited a long time to see the beautiful doctor and to gaze upon her hypnotic blue eyes. He stalked her as she

opened up the car door and got out with her small Chihuahua puppy in her hand.

Without warning, Doc burst out from his hiding spot and rushed her. He placed a knife to her neck and instructed her to open the door and walk inside. She was petrified and didn't understand why her life was filled with this type of drama. She had lost her only and beloved daughter; and the grief was still as strong as it had ever been and now she was being attacked yet again.

Dr. Trussell felt forced to follow her attacker's instruction and so she used her key and opened up the front door. As they entered the house Doc told her to cut on the lights. When she did she got her first glimpse of the man that had been hell bent on killing her.

"Randy, what are you doing here," she screamed. Doc didn't respond immediately. Instead he lunged towards her and grabbed her throat. He began to choke the life out of her as she dropped her dog to the floor. "I'm here to finish what I started," Doc said, as he stared into her eyes. She fought to keep her breath.

Forcefully, Doc threw Dr. Trussell onto the couch and yelled, "Why did you send me to that place?" Dr. Trussell was filled with fear and tearfully replied, "I...I...I only tried to help you." Doc was irate and screamed, "Help me! No, what you wanted to do was destroy me! You wanted to erase any memory of me! That's what you wanted!"

Dr. Trussell was speechless. She could see the fury coming from Doc's eyes as he approached her. He didn't hesitate as he ripped off her clothes and slapped the words from her mouth when she tried to scream for help. He took her shirt and tightly tied her hands behind her back.

"Now I'm going to finish what I started some time ago," he said calmly. "It was you who tried to rape me," she asked surprised, but knowing now it all made sense.

"Yes, it was me," he said, as he threw her from the couch onto the floor.

The dog ran through the house barking and Doc ignored the pooch as he began to sodomize Dr. Trussell. The more she cried and pleaded with him to stop, the greater pleasure he got from having his penis in her ass. When he finished with her rear he turned her over onto her stomach and began to ram himself inside of her vagina. She was in complete pain and felt disgusted; as well as overrun with fear. She didn't know what Doc was going to do next. He was in total control of her body and she was now his slave.

When Doc was finished raping her, he tied up her ankles with a pair of socks and walked into the kitchen. He quickly returned to Dr. Trussell carrying a large knife in his hand.

"Please, Please, Please Randy don't kill me," she begged. Doc ignored her pleading and mounted the woman as he stabbed her repeatedly. As the knife pierced the flesh and the blood splattered onto Doc, he began to get a bigger erection. He had never felt more turned on and was enjoying the melody of her screams.

When the work of killing was done, Doc began to brew up a stew. He chopped pieces of Dr. Trussell up and placed them inside of a large cooking pot. He had gotten tired of the barking dog, so just for fun he stabbed her pet to death and boiled him whole in a large pot too.

As the stew brew on the stove Doc returned to the mangled body of Dr. Trussell and began to enjoy another round of sex with her. She felt good to him when she was alive but in death her mangled corpse was even better. Doc was in no rush and took as much time as he wanted to with his sweet, blue-eyed, doctor.

Chapter 45
Three Days Later
Philadelphia, PA

After leaving Massachusetts, Doc abandoned and torched Dr. Winston's car in Camden, New Jersey. It was at that time he decided to relocate and try to start his life in Philadelphia. He had money from his mother's insurance policy and decided to by a small row home in the West Philadelphia section of the city. The neighborhood was predominantly black but Doc felt very comfortable in the area. He wanted to stay away from Caucasians because he had no trust in them after they had tried to house him in a mental institution for the rest of his life.

Doc begin to start the process of making his house the home that would best suit him. He began to install hidden security cameras within and around his house, and he hired a contractor to build him a laboratory, exam room, and a private office. In addition to the work he was having done, he purchased over ten thousand dollars in medical equipment. He sought out all types of medication and purchased items off the black-market from Canada and Mexico to complete his home office.

The buzz of the new neighbor spread through the neighborhood and many of the people who had heard about Doc wanted to know what he was doing in their hood. They had heard he had a make-shift doctor's office and those without medical insurance made their way to his door to see if he could help them.

Doc welcomed all his new found patients who didn't ask to see a medical license. He was able to treat people who hadn't seen a doctor in years and only took small donations from those who could afford to give; those who couldn't give a dime were still treated. Many people had taken a liking to the new figure on the block,

but there were others who were skeptical about him. No one knew where he came from or what his angle was. He never talked to his patients about his former life and when he was finished fixing up his clients, he would go back to being the private individual that he was.

Doc was an enigma and there was no one around him that could figure him out. His new work brought him lots of satisfaction but his sexual urges still burned deep within. Since he didn't want to bring any unwanted attention to his makeshift practice, he controlled himself. He was starting a new life and he had to calm the beast within him or at least he'd have to have his fun far away from his new home.

Chapter 46
1986
Two Years Later

Annie was beautifully dressed as she walked into the lobby of the Hilton Hotel. She was wearing a tight fitted dress along with a pair of five inch heels. Once she noticed the guy she had come to meet she quickly approached him.

"Hey Ace," she said ever so sexy, as she sat down on the empty seat beside him. "I been waiting on you pretty lady. You ready," Ace asked. "Ready when you are," she said as Ace paid his bar tab.

The two stood up and walked towards the hotel's elevators. Once inside Ace pressed the button for the sixth floor and momentarily they arrived at their stop. They walked to room 628 and hurried into the suite.

Ace a well-known drug dealer from South Philly was short, cocky, and had a smooth brown complexion with a short haircut. He loved to pay prostitutes for sex because he felt he had control over them and when the act was done there were no strings attached.

"Get undressed. I want you now," Ace demanded as Annie followed his instructions. Annie knew exactly how to turn on the man who was paying her, and she slowly removed her clothing as Ace watched without looking away. Despite drugs being a part of her daily routine, her body was still very curvaceous and Ace was lusting for his paid whore.

Ace walked up to Annie, and as he began to touch her breast she said, "Not yet big boy. I need the cash first." Ace was used to the routine and went inside of his pocket and pulled out a thick roll of money. He peeled off five hundred dollars and said, "Here." Annie rushed to place the money into her pocketbook. When she had, Annie

looked at Ace and said, "Now you can do whatever you want to this good, juicy, pink pussy,"

Ace quickly undressed as pre-cum dripped from his dick. Annie climbed on top of the king sized bed and spread her legs far apart.

"The condoms are over there," she said, pointing to the knight stand. Ace rushed to get the condom and quickly placed one onto his erect penis. He jumped onto the bed and rushed inside of her. He could wait no more as he pounded her pussy. Ace was a possessed man as he went nonstop for the next fifty-two minutes. He wanted all of his moneys' worth.

"Turn around bitch! Hurry up, turn around," he shouted as she rushed to lie on her stomach. She arched her back and spread her legs open as Ace positioned himself behind her. She didn't notice that Ace had slipped off the condom as he began to penetrate her deeply and more intensely.

As the warmth and wetness of her pussy intensified he could go no longer as he gave in and bussed deep inside of Annie. For a few minutes he kept her propped up and stayed inside. Then he slowly pulled out as his dick's sensitivity intensified upon removal from her pussy. He then pretended to remove the condom and tossed it to the floor. Within twenty minutes Ace was knocked out on the bed in a deep sleep.

Annie began to quietly dress. She knew that Ace had lots of cash on him and she went into his pockets as he slept without notice. She also took his gold watch from off of the nightstand and slipped it into her pocketbook. Once her mission was complete she walked out of the hotel room with ten thousand dollars in cash and an expensive gold watch.

Instead of taking the elevator she took the steps because she knew if Ace woke up he'd be on her tail.

When Annie got outside she walked into the hotel's parking lot and got into the car with Sonny.

"Here Daddy," she said, as she passed him all the money she had stolen. "Jackpot," Sonny shouted, as he pulled off. "Do you think he's going to come after me. He's not like the other guys I've taken money from," Annie fearfully asked. "Fuck that trick," Sonny said. "But he hustles Daddy and they can get crazy," she said.

Sonny stopped his car at a green light and held up traffic as the cars behind him blew their horns for him to move on. "Fuck all them goddamn tricks. If he wants to come and get dealt with then I'll deal with him then, but you don't worry about shit that ain't your business. I got this, you understand," Sonny said. "Yes Daddy. I got it," Annie replied.

For the past few months Annie and Sonny had been plotting and setting guys up to get robbed. She knew what they were doing was dangerous, but she was too afraid of the consequences she would suffer if she didn't go along with Sonny's plans.

"Did you find me anymore bitches," Sonny asked, as he pulled up into McDonald's parking lot. "Yes. I'm meeting up with a new girl tomorrow and she's supposed to bring a friend," Annie said. "Good cause we need a few more bitches to help take this game to a higher level. The more bitches we got the more money I make," Sonny said, as they got out of the car and walked inside of the fast food restaurant.

Chapter 47

Inside of his office, Doc sat around looking at photos. He had pictures of naked, mutilated, female corpses taped to his private office walls. His body was covered in blood as he sat in a trance. Just a few feet away from him he had a nude, unconscious female strapped to a long operating table. The unsuspecting girl was a young prostitute named Gia and she had been locked in Doc's basement for three days.

Doc had begun to have fun with her, having cut off both nipples and removing her eyes. Her mouth was covered in thick duct tape as he mutilated the woman to keep her from screaming, but the pain and shock of the horrors being done to her made her pass out. Gia was trapped and being used exclusively for Doc's pleasure and there was nothing she could do about it.

Doc stood up from his seat and approached his newest victim. He ripped the tape from her mouth, causing her to be hastily awakened to her reality.

"I'm sorry," Doc whispered into Gia's ear. "Please don't kill me," she cried out. Doc climbed on top of her naked body as she trembled in fear. "You didn't know," Doc asked. "Know what," Gia cried. "That you're already dead," Doc said, as he pulled out his switchblade and slit the young girl's throat.

Doc smiled as he watched her bleed out and suffocate on her own blood. He then became angry with himself as he said, "You shouldn't have killed her! You said you were going to stop!!! Okay this is the last one."

There was an evil inside of Doc that could not be stopped. No matter what good he did for his new community, the thirst for murder and to torture people overrode his best intentions. This man was a sociopath and a serial killer living in the heart of the ghetto.

Chapter 48
The Next Day

Sonny parked his car on the corner of 19th and Christian Streets. He looked at Annie and said, "Alright bitch you hurry up and see what's up with them hoes so we can get back to the hotel." She quickly said, "Okay Daddy. I'll be right back," as she rushed from the car.

Annie had planned to meet two young girls she had met at a night club a week earlier. She was on a desperate mission to recruit as many girls for her Daddy as she could. He wanted more girls on their roster and she didn't want to disappoint him.

When she got to the home of the young lady she was meeting, she knocked on the door. "Hey come on in," someone said, as Annie turned the knob and walked into the house. An attractive redbone was sitting in a chair in the living room reading Jet Magazine as a beautiful brown sister approached Annie.

"Hey girl. Annie this is my girlfriend Pam that I told you about," Veronica said. "Yes, she's pretty just like you said," Annie said. "So what's up? I don't have much time I need to get back to my son," Pamela asked as she put down the magazine. "I came here to offer you two a piece of a generous pie without hardly any risk," Annie said. "Oh yeah, well how do we get parts of this pie," Pamela interrupted. My man and I been taking these well paid drug dealers to different hotels in the city and getting them for all they got. I use my pussy or give them one of these pills and then I rob them blind. It's easy. They fall asleep and you take everything they got on them. It's just that simple," Annie said.

"But what if they don't fall asleep," Veronica asked. "No, they all fall asleep. This pill makes sure of it and it's our job to make sure we lace their drinks before

we get them back to the hotel room. We need them passed the fuck out so we can get in and out without them having a fucking clue. I'm telling you this shit is sweet and if anything goes wrong Sonny will always be waiting outside for us," Annie said.

Pamela stood up and said, "So let me get this straight. We have to drug these niggaz, fuck them, and then rob them when they fall asleep. Then afterwards we meet up with Sonny and give him the money." Annie looked at her and said, "That's right." Pamela quickly asked, "Well how much do we get." Veronica was thinking the same thing as she crossed her arms and she said, "Yes, how much do I get to keep?"

Annie looked at the young ladies and said, "Sonny gives you twenty percent of the take." They both stared at each other and then Pam asked, "So we fuck these niggas, rob them, and give him all the money just to get a twenty percent cut?" Annie looked at Pamela and tried to convince her that the deal made sense and said, "Yes but he finds all the tricks and protects us. He takes us to the hotels and he makes sure everything is okay."

"Hell I ain't selling my pussy for nobody to give me a cut when I'm doing all the work. I can just fuck a nigga and keep all my cash. I'm not interested," Pamela said. "What about you Veronica," Annie asked. "Well I don't know. Give me a few days and I'll call you."

Annie was frustrated. She knew that Sonny was going to be extremely upset if she hadn't gotten at least one of the girls on his roster. She tried to make the deal sound sweeter by telling them how much money she was making and all the things she had recently bought, but Pamela didn't budge and Veronica was still on the fence. So, instead of continuing to push, she shook their hands and left.

"Girl you better not play yourself. You're too beautiful of a woman to fall for that scam. You're smart enough to figure this out for yourself and if you want to make money, then you need to be your own boss. That plan she was selling sounds like you're about to be pimped out, and Ronnie we don't do that," Pamela said.

Veronica looked at her friend and took a deep breath and on the exhale she said, "I feel you but I'm broke! It's hard as hell out here and I just need to make some fast money. The only thing I got going on right now is this face and this sexy ass body." Pamela interrupted her before she could go on and said, "Girl that's more than enough. It's bitches out here with less than that and they getting major checks from these tricks. I got a six year old son and I'll be damned if I lay with someone and then give all my money to some pimp; and I don't trust that bitch Annie no way. Fuck no. Stop thinking small. Quit fucking with these drugs dealers, pimps, and low class hustlers and start dealing with the professionals."

Veronica was listening. She wanted to know more and asked, "Like who, Pam?" Her friend was ready to give her the knowledge she needed to move pass the low grade men she had been sleeping with. "Like a lawyer, judges, politicians, and even professional athletics with guaranteed contracts. These guys will give you more money and you deserve it. You need to be treated and I'm not judging you, but I'm saying if you're gonna fuck for money you mind as well make it worth it," Pamela said, as they both laughed in agreement.

Veronica sat in deep thought. She knew she had just been given some good game and she needed to get to the money. She needed to connect herself with the right folks so that she could build a solid clientele and be her own boss.

Chapter 49

"Bitch you can't do nothin right," Sonny yelled as she slapped Annie's face. "We need a few more bitches and you can't convince a hoe to get down with the program," he said, as he slapped the other side of her face. Annie held her face with her hands as she said, "Daddy, I swear I told them how sweet the deal was but they didn't bite." Sonny ignored her. All he wanted to hear was that he had two more girls to add to his roster so he could hook bigger fish with more money.

"Did you hear from Gia," Sonny asked as he drove down Washington Avenue. "No. Not yet. It's like she disappeared from the face of the earth because I haven't seen or heard from her," Annie said, as she rubbed her now bruised and stinging face. "And you didn't see the trick she rolled with either," he asked. "No I was on the opposite side of the street handling my business, but he looked like he was Puerto Rican or something. I couldn't really see," she said. "Damn I hope that hoe ain't run off with some trick. If I see her ass again I'mma put my foot up her ass so far that it's gonna leave a footprint in her stomach!" Annie didn't think Gia had run away. She didn't have the nerve to.

"Maybe something happened to her. You know it's some crazy people out here," Annie said. Sonny pulled his car over and parked near 32nd Street and Greys Ferry Avenue. "Listen here hoe that bitch Gia ain't nothing but a money stealing hoe! She's been stealing and keeping money from me for years. She out here fucking and keeping all my goddamn money to get high," Sonny said.

Annie listened as Sonny vented out all of his frustrations. She knew when he got this angry it was best for her to keep her mouth shut or he'd put his fist in it. Inside, she was filled with frustration because she hated

Sonny. She may have camouflaged her feelings and kept in line with his requirement but she hated him, nonetheless. He had seen her coming, and like a predator, he scouted his weak prey when she got off of that greyhound bus years ago. He had taken control over her life and forcefully filled her body with poison until she was hooked. He had become her father, pimp, provider, and he ruled her life. This was not a man but a monster, and when she tried to rid herself of him he beat a fear inside of her that kept her a prisoner, even without the chains.

When Sonny pulled off a tear fell from Annie's eyes and she quickly wiped it away before he could see it. While she was hiding her pain, there was another person playing hide and go seek with Sonny. He was being followed by an enemy from his past and he was watching every move that Sonny made. When the time was right he would make his move and strike with lethal force.

Chapter 50
Later That Night

Wearing a pair of surgical gloves and a black jumpsuit, Doc dragged Gia's corpse into a small, empty alley. The passageway was filled with broken beer bottles, trash and a pungent smell filled the air. Doc laid her body down and started to walk out of the alley but was frozen in his tracks when he saw the blinking lights of a police car. He was caught, he thought, as he tried to think of a way to explain why he was in an alley with a dead prostitute. He had thought of the idea of being jailed and it didn't sit well with him. He could hear footsteps as they approached the alley and he took off running in the opposite direction.

"Hey you," the officer yelled out when he saw Doc running and the dead body lying on the ground. Doc didn't stop. He knew the alley. He knew the city. He had studied the streets and had an advantage over the cop.

The officer drew his .38 pistol and started to chase Doc as he screamed for him to stop running. Doc continued to run through the streets at an accelerated pace. He never looked back until he had gotten within a block of his home. To his surprise he had outrun the officer. So he dashed over to his backyard fence and entered the house through the backdoor. Within seconds he was watching the police activity on his hidden camera system that was taking place outside of his home and in the area. The cops were desperate to find the man who had just killed a young woman. They had looked high and low but the trail had gone cold when the officer failed to catch the man who had outrun him.

Later that evening as Doc lay in his bed, he watched the news as the anchor described the happenings of the day.

"Earlier tonight a female was found in a dark alleyway. The woman's body appeared to be mutilated and sexually assaulted before being killed and dumped in the dark back alley in West Philadelphia. The victim has been identified as twenty-three year old Gia Chambers, who was a former temple student and resident of the Germantown section of the city.

Police say they are looking for a suspect who is an African American male with very fair skin. He stands about 5'10 and weighs around 165 pounds. He was last seen running from the scene and police are asking if you have any knowledge of who this individual may be that you call 9-1-1 immediately."

Doc smiled and the room became brighter. He had gotten away with murder and the escape gave him a thrill like no other; but the chase had worn him out. He cut off the television and looked at the picture of his mother on his nightstand and said, "I love you Marabella. No woman will ever replace you." Then ever so peacefully he drifted off to sleep.

Chapter 51
West Philly
The Blue Moon Motel

With both eyes shut, Sonny sat back in his chair and enjoyed the pleasing sensations he was getting from Annie's soft and juicy lips. WDAS was playing a new hit from the R&B Diva, Anita Baker. Sonny played the radio to mute out the constant commotion that went on outside of the broken down motel room.

The Blue Moon was the stomping ground for pimps, prostitutes, tricks and pesky drug addicts. Sonny had grown up just a few blocks from the hotel and he knew the area well. The motel was nothing to brag about but the money Sonny made off of this location kept him thriving in his business, so he stayed put.

A yellow cab pulled up directly in front of the motel. The male passenger instructed the cab driver to wait for him and with the guarantee of an additional fifty dollars, on top of what he was already paid for the ride, the driver kept the car in park.

Once the male was inside of the building he pulled out his 9mm handgun from his jacket and rushed down the hallway until he got in front of room 107. He didn't wait as he stepped back from the door and kicked it down. When the door burst open the man rushed into the room and began to beat Sonny with his gun as Annie screamed. The more he struck Sonny, the quieter Annie got. The man didn't stop until Sonny had stopped moving and when he was done Annie had become as quiet as a mouse.

"Please Ace don't kill me," Annie pleaded as she saw the man she had robbed for ten thousand dollars and a gold watch. He stared at her as anger filled his eyes. He approached Annie and began to beat her with his gun as well. Being a female made no difference to him. He

showed her no mercy and kept beating her until blood covered her face and she could no longer speak.

With both parties unconscious, bloody and on the floor, Ace stood over Sonny's body and before he could pull the trigger he heard someone coming towards the room. Ace struck Sonny in the head with his gun once more and then tucked his gun away. He then ran from the room straight for his cab. He jumped into the car with blood on his hands and blood splattered on his clothes and screamed, "Get me out of her now!" The driver asked no questions and pulled off immediately.

Inside of the room, the motionless bodies of Sonny and Annie lay covered in blood. Ace had gotten his vengeance and even though he had not killed them, he surely sent a message. He was not about to be taken by no pimp and his hoe, and if either ever tried anything like that again the next time would be worse.

Two men who had heard the screams and had saw Ace running from the room, entered to see what had happened. When they saw the two on the floor, one of the men told the other to call the cops. As soon as Sonny heard that, he spoke. "No, don't call no cops. We alright." He tried to get up off the floor but was only able to lift up his head. Annie was struggling to breath and Sonny asked one of the men, "Listen I need y'all to get me to that hood doctor. I'll pay y'all but no cops and I can't go in the regular hospital, you dig."

The men agreed as they struggled to get both parties up from off the floor and onto the bed. One man left the room and went to get his car ready as the other helped Sonny wipe his face. Once Sonny was on the bed he was able to sit up. As he wiped the blood from his mouth he said, "I'mma kill that mutherfucka," as he looked over at Annie who still hadn't regained consciousness.

Chapter 52

On the corner of 48th and Sampson Streets, a tinted black Ford pulled up and parked behind a brand new silver Cadillac. A tall Caucasian male exited his car and walked over to the black man who was sitting inside of his Cadillac. His eyes scanned the area before he opened the passenger car door and got inside.

"What's up Hood? Word is you're doing real good out here on these streets ever since Big Greg got murdered. I hear you're the man now," the white man said. Hood looked at him and said, "Thanks for putting two bullets in the back of his head Detective Perry." The detective smiled and said, "No problem boss man. As long as the money is right, you don't have to worry about a damn thing."

Detective Ron Perry was the most ruthless, crooked cop on the Philadelphia Police force. For the right amount of money he'd kill anyone, and he used the power behind his badge to get away with it. For a little over a year he had been on Hood's payroll; and his duties were to shakedown, extort, and if necessary kill off the competition.

Hood passed Ron Perry a brown paper bag that was filled with five thousand dollars in cash and said, "I'm going to need you again real soon." Ron looked at his employer and asked "What's wrong," as he heard the seriousness in his tone. "I just need you to stay on point because there are a lot of changes I'm going to need you to make. I can't have nothing and no one standing in my way."

The detective looked at Hood and said, "No worries. I've got you covered. Oh and did you hear about the girl that got killed in the alley," he asked. Hood kept quiet as Ron spoke. "She was council member Steve

Chamber's daughter and the force is on this one. Anything you know of or have heard can help us shut this case down. She was a runaway, and I don't know what happened at home, but she got caught up in these streets, and it cost the girl her life. So if you hear anything let me know," Ron said. "I don't know her but if I hear something I'll let you know," Hood lied. "Thanks. There's a killer on the loose so be careful out here," Ron said, as he shook Hood's hand and began to get out of the car. "A killer...that's the least of my worriers," Hood said, as he began to laugh.

Chapter 53

Shocked to his core, Doc stood over Annie's bruised and beaten body. He could not believe that his best friend, the young girl that he had always hoped to see, was finally in front of him, but the current circumstances were not how he envisioned their reunion.

Sonny and Annie had been dropped off to the doctor by two good Samaritans from the motel. Doc had patched up Sonny and given him a few pain meds. His injuries were minor. His nose was broken, a few of his teeth had been knocked out, and he'd have to sport a 6inch scar across his forehead until it healed. When he was all cleaned up, Sonny told Doc he'd be back in a few days to pick up Annie, before he placed a few hundred dollars on the table and left out the door.

Doc turned his focus on his friend. She was pretty messed up. Her retina had been damaged, her nose and ribs were broken, and she had a large contusion on her head. She had yet to awaken from her comatose state but Doc refused to leave her side until she opened up her eyes.

Nervously he paced the floor, waiting for the moment she would say something to him. He had placed an IV line into her arm to give her fluids. She was severely dehydrated and as he looked at her arms he could tell she was a regular heroin user. He hated the fact that she had injected that poison into her veins. He just could not believe that the one person in the world who he cared for, who had accepted him and understood him, had fallen into such a decrepit state of life.

Several hours had passed and Annie finally began to utter sounds. She struggled to open her eyes and when she finally regained vision, she was dazed and confused by her surroundings; until she noticed a very familiar face staring down at her. "Randy...oh my...Randy is that you,"

she softly uttered. "Yes Annie. It's me," Doc said. "What are you doing here," she asked. "I live here. I'm a doctor and you're in my exam room," he said, as he softly rubbed her shoulder. "You're a doctor," she asked, still not fully sure of what had happened to her. "Yes I am," he confirmed. "That's great. That's what you always wanted to be. Randy, how did I get here," Annie asked. "Someone brought you and your male friend here but he left in a silver Cadillac. He said to look out for you and he'll be back soon," Doc said.

"Okay. That's his friend Hood. Sonny works for him," Annie said. "Oh okay. Is Sonny your husband," Doc asked. "No," Annie smiled. "He's...he's my pimp," Annie said feeling embarrassed. "Your Pimp," Doc shouted. "Yes. I've been with him ever since I got back to Philly. He took me in and he's taking care of me," she said.

Doc's blue eyes were filled with rage. He grabbed Annie's arm and said, "Is he the reason for this," as he looked at the track marks on her limb. "Randy, it's hard out here and sometimes I need an escape from my life. Everyone can't become a doctor. I had to do what I had to do," she said, as a flow of tears ran from her eyes.

"You didn't answer my question. Is he the person that put this poison in your system," Doc said, demanding a response. "Yes Randy! Yes! He gave me the drugs," she shouted as a part of her tainted soul began to cleanse itself. "Why Annie? Why did you let this loser ruin your life? You're better than this," Doc said. "Randy, he runs my life. I can't get away from him, because I tried that before and he almost killed me! I'm scared of him! He's dangerous and there's nothing I can do to change my life now," she said.

Doc's rage had intensified as he looked at his friend and said, "Annie I've changed a lot. There is a lot about me you might not want to know but I'm not afraid

of Sonny. I can make people disappear and no matter what you say he's going to get out of your life for good."

Sonny had taken his best friend and turned her into a heroin-shooting-whore. He had Annie brainwashed and under his full control, but Doc didn't scare easily. Sonny had a debt to pay for what he had done to Annie and Doc was ready to collect.

Chapter 54
Two Days Later

On the corner of 19th and Tasker Streets, Ron Perry sat inside of his black Ford Taurus and watched as a police officer did a routine traffic stop on a man in a red Mercedes Benz. He watched as the officer cuffed the male and placed him in the back of the squad car. As the officer returned to his driver seat and pulled off, Ron Perry began to follow them.

Ten minutes later the police car drove around the back of a dilapidated warehouse on Snyder Avenue and parked.

"What the fuck is going on," the scared man asked, as he sat in the backseat. The black Taurus had now pulled up and parked beside the police cruiser. Ron Perry exited his vehicle with his loaded .38 in hand and the man shouted, "Yo what the fuck is up!" Neither gave his words any attention and Ron turned to the officer and said, "I got it from here," as he passed the officer an envelope. Ron Perry escorted the man from the back of the police car and the officer pulled off.

"Come the fuck on Ace," Ron said, as he forced him into the abandoned warehouse. Once they were inside Ace stomach filled with death and he pleaded with Ron for his life. Ron was quiet as he continued to walk Ace deeper into the run down building. When they had stopped walking, Ace was shocked to see Hood and the recently battered Sonny.

"Please Hood. I got a three year old daughter man. Please man he and his bitched robbed me and I couldn't let that shit go, man I'm a man first. That shit wasn't cool. I'm just trying to make it out here, come on Hood don't do this," Ace pleaded. "You should have thought about staying alive before you fucked up one of my workers,"

Hood said. "Shut the fuck up you coward," Sonny yelled, as Ace continued to plead for his life.

Ronny Perry stood back as he smiled and smoked on his Newport cigarette, and then he said, "Can we get this shit over with already."

Hood pulled out a hunter's blade that could very well slice through wood with ease. He handed the blade to Sonny and said, "Nigga, handle that." Sonny walked over to Ace who had tears falling from his eyes, as he fell to the floor and pleaded for his life. Sonny slid the sharp knife into Ace's throat and then he slowly pulled the knife back and forth as Ace's blood escaped from the now gabbing wound. He felt no remorse and no guilt as he continued to cut open flesh and to rip through veins.

Ace's body fell to the floor. He was no more. The men stood in the warehouse feeling untouchable and willing to repeat the act should anyone else try to stand in their way. Hood was the leader and he used his powers to keep his empire growing. He ruled the streets and he wouldn't let anyone challenge his rule, even if someone in his camp had fucked up. Ace found that out the hard way.

Chapter 55
A Week Later

Days had passed and Sonny finally returned to Doc's door. The swelling on his face had gone down and his pain was manageable. Annie had gotten better and after a week with Doc the two had strengthened their bond. While Annie was with Doc, he had taken care of her as if she was a child. He fed her, bathed her, and had given her a small dose of heroin to keep her from getting sick. The drug was so addictive that the withdrawal symptoms were often worse than the continued use.

While Annie was in his home, Doc never had his usual rages for sex or the thirst to kill. He was at peace and happy to care for his friend. Annie didn't know about his demented ways and her memory from their childhood, when he had confessed that he had murdered people, had long faded away. He was her knight in shining armor. He had helped her become functional again.

Doc stood on his porch and watched as Annie walked over to Sonny's car. "Thanks for everything Randy. I love you," Annie said as she waved goodbye. "Bitch get your ass in this damn car we got money to make," Sonny demanded. "Hey Doc, I'll be back to look out for you man. You did good by me and I always pay my debts," Sonny said. "Okay. Please don't forget about me," Doc said.

Sonny raced out of the parking spot to get Annie back onto the strip. She was his money maker and he wanted her working the streets immediately.

Doc walked back into his home and suddenly he felt empty and alone. He couldn't wait to see his friend again because she brought him a pleasure he hadn't felt in such a long time. Doc then walked into his office and pulled out some photos that were hidden in the back of his

file cabinet. The photos were of naked female corpses he had taken down the day Annie and Sonny came.

The sight of the photos awoke the beast inside of him. His sexual hunger deepened and he wanted to taste flesh. To calm himself down he used his familiar method of masturbation. After the first time he ejaculated, he came two more times; still his erection would not go down.

Doc cleaned himself off and put on his coat and his gloves. It was cold outside but not too cold for hunting. Tonight was a night to kill and tonight Doc would get himself a good prize.

Chapter 56
Later That Night

Disappointed and with his head held low, Doc walked back into his home. He had been out all night looking for prey but came up empty handed. As soon as he removed his coat and sat down the door bell rung. He rushed to his video monitor to see who the unexpected guest was. When he saw the face of the visitor he began to smile and he rushed to the door.

"Wassup Doc, what you forgot about me," Sonny said. "No, I didn't forget. Come on in," Doc replied. "Here's the money and thanks for everything," Sonny said, as he passed Doc a sealed envelope. "How's Annie," Doc asked. "She's okay. Her ass is back on the track where she belongs," Sonny laughed. "The tracks," Doc said confused. "Yeah, Annie is a whore, Doc. She works for me, and when she's out on the streets, we call that the track. That's my bitch and she makes me a lot of money. That's how I get to drive these fancy cars and wear these fly ass clothes, you dig," Sonny said. "Oh wow. She must be really good," Doc asked. "The best! Let me know when you want to try that thing out and I'll give you a lil discount," Sonny said grinning.

"How are your wounds," Doc asked, changing the subject. "Man funny you should ask, cause I've been having crazy headaches. Shit is killin me," Sonny said. "Well, I have something downstairs that can take care of that. Something real strong that will take all your pain away. Follow me," Doc said as he led Sonny into the basement.

Once they were downstairs Doc's mind filled with a devious plot as he looked through the shelves for the perfect fix for Sonny.

"Have a seat," Doc said. Sonny sat down and relaxed. "You got a lot of stuff down here Doc. This shit looks like a real damn doctor's office," Sonny said. "Thanks Sonny," Doc said as he took a syringe out of one of his drawers. "What's up with all these dead chicks in these pictures," Sonny asked, as he stared at the photos completely affixed to them.

Doc noticed his wall of dead women had Sonny's full attention. Slowly he began creeping towards him as he held a long syringe in his right hand.

"Ahhh!!! What the hell," Sonny screamed as Doc plunged the syringe deep into his neck. Doc stepped back and watched Sonny remove the needle from his neck. Sonny stood but the narcotics rushed into his nervous system and began to scramble its signals. He began to stagger and did his best to keep his feet planted on the ground, but the paralysis was taking a hold of his body.

Doc had injected Sonny with a powerful drug called Succinylcholine Chloride-Sux for short. This was a neuromuscular paralytic drug that would paralyze all the muscles inside of your body instantaneously. Anyone injected with the drug without the use of a ventilator support would surely die. The medication makes it impossible for you to breathe on your own, and you would be conscious as you suffocate to death. Succinylcholine Chloride is so powerful that it's one of the three drugs used for executions by lethal injection.

Doc watched as Sonny's body was overtaken by the substance and he hit the ground hard. Sonny struggled to speak and the only thing that exited his mouth was thick white salvia. His eyes were wide open as he tried his best to beg for help but he could not speak. Doc had him right where he wanted him.

"You like pimping hoes. I think I might make you my bitch tonight," Doc said as he lifted Sonny up off the floor and lay him face down on his exam table.

Doc pulled down Sonny's pants and after placing on a condom he mounted him and fucked him hard in his ass. He was vicious and gave the dying man no break as he continued to ram his hard dick into his ass.

"Who's the bitch now," Doc screamed as he continued pounding Sonny's virgin anus. Sonny could do nothing as his body began to shut down due to lack of oxygen. Doc didn't concern himself with the fate of Sonny. He continued to let out his sexual frustrations upon the pimp.

When Doc had had his fill of Sonny's ass, he removed himself and went back to his closet to get something very special for the man who had harmed his best friend. Within minutes, Doc returned to Sonny's lifeless body holding a machete in his hand. He began to hack at Sonny's neck. With each whack he shouted, "This is for Annie," until he had severed his head from his body.

Afterwards, Doc placed the head into a plastic bag and placed it in his deep freezer. Doc then poured acid onto Sonny's body and his flesh deteriorated. Then, while wearing protective gloves, he placed his headless body into a body bag.

It was late evening and no one was out. Doc placed the body bag inside of Sonny's car and pulled off. He drove the car to 22nd Street and Hunting Park Avenue and parked it there. He looked around as he pulled his hoody over his head and quickly got out of the vehicle. He made his way back to his home in West Philly where he sat on the couch and felt pleased with his work. He had freed his friend Annie and gotten his much needed fix as well.

Chapter 57
Three Days Later

Ron Perry parked his black Ford on the corner of 52nd and Walnut Streets. Moments later, Hood pulled up and parked behind him. Ron rushed out of his car and got inside of Hood's new red BMW.

"What the hell did they say, how the hell did he die," Hood asked. Ron Perry shook his head and said, "His head was off. Somebody cut off his damn head and his body was fucked up. The sick bastard that worked on Sonny fucked him right in his ass, and then he poured acid all over his body. That shit ate right through his flesh. Somebody did him in real good," Ron Perry said.

"Fuck," Hood screamed, as he pounded his fist onto the dashboard. "I want you to find out who did this shit and bring him straight to me," Hood continued. "I'm on it boss man. That's some sick shit and I don't want a psycho fuck like that out on these streets. I've never seen no shit like that. They're calling it the work of a serial killer at headquarters," Ron Perry said. "I don't give a fuck whose behind it, I just want his head," Hood said.

"Ron this shit got me worried. Who don't know that Sonny was untouchable? I mean since this shit happened I've been worried about myself. I've had some fucked up dreams and I'm thinking somebody is out to try me, you know," Hood said. "NO! That's not happening! You're the boss out here and nobody is going to do shit to you on my watch. Just keep alert and let me do what I do. Don't listen to those dreams. I got you," Ron Perry said.

"Okay," Hood said. He still felt uneasy. He felt there was more to the story and somehow the man who had killed Sonny was after him. He just couldn't shake it, but for now, he had to run his town and keep his business together.

Chapter 58
Early The Next Morning

Boom! Boom! Boom! Annie banged on Doc's door as hard as she could. Once he cleared his visitor on his monitor, he rushed to the door to let his friend in. She looked a mess. He could tell she had been getting high all night and hadn't showered or eaten.

"What's wrong Annie," Doc said as he opened his door and let her inside. "Sonny is gone. He's gone Randy," she said. I keep calling him and paging him but he's not answering. I don't know where he is," Annie continued.

Doc grabbed her by the arm and led her to the couch. As she sat down she began to cry. She didn't know what to do without the man who had been her everything; even if that involved a life of chaos and harm. Doc sat down beside his sobbing friend and tried to comfort her.

"Annie, I thought you wanted to get away from Sonny. He's the reason your life is the way it is. He treated you like trash," Doc said. "Randy, I need him. I don't know what to do without him. I've never been without him, and I just need to find him," she cried.

Doc listened to Annie as she sobbed about her pimp. He knew she was brainwashed. Her pimp had been successful with getting into her mind and now she felt an attachment to the monster who shoved poison in her veins and made her sell her body to endless men.

"Annie you don't need Sonny. You never did. What he did to you was wrong and you deserve better. You have suffered a great deal of many pains and I just want to help my friend. Follow me, I have something for you," Doc said, as he took Annie to the deep freezer.

When they came upon the freezer he opened it and ripped opened the bag and said, "Here is your Sonny."

Annie couldn't believe what she was looking at as her eyes grew bigger than they had ever been. "I did this for you, Annie. You needed your freedom and now you have it," Doc said.

"You killed Sonny, Randy," Annie said, still in a state of shock. "Yes. I had to. There was no other way you'd be free from him."

In that moment she reached her arms around Doc and hugged him with all the strength she could muster up. She didn't know how to express her gratitude and as tears fell from her face she said, "Randy, thank you! Thanks so much! I love you." Doc felt relieved that she was not angry and said, "I love you to Annie. I did this for you." She knew that Sonny was connected and she was concerned so she asked, "Does anyone else know about this?" Doc looked at her and proudly said, "No. I know what I'm doing." Annie smiled.

"I need to clean myself up. I look a mess. Is it okay," Annie asked. "Sure, please do. Everything you need is in the bathroom. There's an extra toothbrush in the bathroom closet too."

Doc watched as Annie walked upstairs until she disappeared from his sight. He sat on the sofa and listened to the sound of running water as she showered. He began to think about the feelings he had for his friend. She was the only living person that he loved and would cause no harm to.

"Doc, can you come up here," Annie called out. Doc stood up and nervously walked upstairs. He could hear Annie singing in the shower as he walked into the bathroom. Annie slid open the shower curtain, displaying her body.

"Don't just stand there Randy, get in," Annie instructed, as Doc began to undress. When he was nude he stepped into the shower and let the warm water soothe his

skin. Annie noticed that Doc was becoming excited and she said, "I see you got some black up in you." Next she began to lather up a rag as she began to wash Doc's pale body. When she had gotten him nice and soapy she placed him in front of the showerhead and let the water rinse him clean.

Annie backed her ass up against Doc's erect penis and said, "Randy I want you to fuck me...fuck me good and hard." She then bent over and positioned herself as she inserted Doc's rock hard dick inside of her. Like a skilled professional, Doc fucked Annie as aggressively as he liked, and she enjoyed each second of it.

As the warm water ran down their naked bodies passionate moans filled the air. This was the first time Doc had ever been with a woman who had consented to having sex with him. It felt amazing to him and for over an hour the sadistic killer that lived inside of him was nowhere to be found.

Chapter 59

For the past two months Doc and Annie spent a lot more time together. Although Annie had lost her pimp, she was still tricking. Doc tried his best to get her to leave the street life alone but it was a part of her. Since he knew he couldn't convince her to quit, he kept a close eye on her; which was tough because she moved wherever the tricks were.

Still, they had a bond. Many evenings Annie would come back banging on Doc's door to get a meal, a shower, something to eat and she always gave Doc a piece of her. He loved being with Annie. It was a very strange love affair, but they made it work.

One day while Doc was watching the news the phone rang.

"Hello, he said. "Randy it's me. I need you to bail me out," Annie said. "Again Annie," Doc replied. "Yes! I need a thousand dollars. Come down here and get me out! I can't take it in this place," she shouted. "Okay, Annie. I'm on my way," he said. "Thanks baby. I love you," Annie replied.

After a long sigh, Doc got dressed and headed down to the station. This was the third time Doc had bailed Annie out for prostitution in a month. She was now abusing cocaine and was often too high to realize the undercover officers who watched her selling her body. Doc was sick and tired of the abuse she endured, but the love he had for her would not allow him to let her sit in jail. He had offered to pay for her rehab services but she outright refused to quit cocaine, or prostitution.

Once Annie was released, she returned with Doc to his home. He bathed her; made her something to eat, and then they went into his bedroom to watch television. Again, he approached her with the idea of rehab. "Annie

please get help," Doc pleaded. "Stop wasting your time on me. I'm fine. I have everything under control and I'll pay you back the money as soon as I get on my feet," she said, as she laid her nude body flat onto the bed. "Annie you can't pay me back. You're always locked up or high. You should just quit," Doc said. "Randy enough talking! Just lay back and let's enjoy ourselves."

Annie reached for the remote control and cut off the television. She undressed Doc, and then she pushed him back on the bed. Annie mounted him and gave him the ride of his lifetime. He couldn't resist her and for the moment he would enjoy being sexually teased, pleased, and satisfied by her, and worry about Annie's problem later.

Chapter 60
1987
Six Months Later

Ron Perry had been assigned to investigate the cold cases of ten women. In the west and north sections of the city all the victims they found had been raped and brutally murdered. It was clear to Ron and the people on the special victim's team, that they were looking for a serial killer; but they didn't have one clue to lead them to the suspect. The killer was meticulous and covered his tracks. Ron always suspected that the person behind the killings had some form of medical training because of the incisions they made. They were clean and not the works of an amateur.

Doc's Residence

Sitting inside of his office, Doc was reading a book entitled Egyptian Philosophy and Medicine. Lately, Doc had become obsessed with the Egyptians, Chinese and African medical beliefs and techniques. As he read the book he was astonished to learn how precise the Egyptians were when they removed organs; especially the heart. He loved the heart and how that one organ could shut down the entire body. He read for hours and even with all the knowledge he had found, he was still in amazement at its power.

Suddenly, Doc put his precious book down. He got up and walked over to the naked woman whom he had strapped down on his operating table. For three days he had been torturing her and raping her. He had recently removed her blue eyes and they were in a glass jar with another pair of eyes.

"Why are you doing this to me," the woman said. She was unable to see and her spirit was drained. She wanted to die but there was a strength inside of her that would not allow her to ask him to hurry up and kill her. She kept hope that maybe one day he would let her go.

"I have to learn from you. You should be honored to dedicate yourself to the advancement of medicine," Doc said, as he inserted a liquid filled syringe into her neck.

The woman began to shake and tremble, which was not the outcome Doc wanted. "Don't die on me you bitch! Don't you die," Doc screamed at the woman. Her heartbeat raced and Doc became irritated with her. He had been preparing her for open heart surgery and he wanted to remove the heart while she was alive. Doc had miscalculated her dosage and given her too much. So instead of being able to perform his procedure on a live patient, the tormented woman died on the operating table.

Chapter 61
Early The Next Morning

The loud banging at the door woke Doc up from his peaceful sleep. He rushed to look at the small video monitor by his bed and quickly jumped up. After placing his robe on, he rushed downstairs to answer the door.

"Annie, where have you been," Doc asked, as she walked into the house. "Randy, we have a problem," she said. "What's wrong? Are you okay," the concerned man asked. "No, I'm not okay," she said sitting down on the sofa. "Well what is it," Doc said, becoming impatient. "I'm pregnant with your child Randy," Annie blurted out. "What," Doc said shocked. "Yes. You're the only man I've been with without protection. I'm pregnant with your child and this is not good for business. Hood's been on my case about me being tired all the time and this is the last thing he wants to hear right now," Annie said.

"Fuck Hood," Doc shouted. "I don't know what to do Randy," Annie said, as tears fell from her brown eyes.

Doc paced the floor. He was livid. The woman he loved was pregnant with his child and she was out on the streets selling her body and using drugs. She had ended up working for Hood, and Doc just didn't understand why the streets had a hold on his woman. This was not what he wanted for Annie or his unborn child.

"Annie, we need to get away from Philadelphia, Just you and me. This is not a good place for you. You need help getting off of those drugs because if you don't they will kill you one day," Doc pleaded. "Randy I'll be fine. I'm going to figure this out but right now I need some money," she said.

Doc reached into his pocket and gave her a hundred dollars, and no sooner than he had Annie was out

the door. All he could do was shake his head in disbelief. He hoped that he'd hear from her real soon.

As soon as Annie left Doc, she rushed to a neighborhood crack house and stood in line. The crack epidemic was devastating the city; especially the poor people in the ghetto. It hit them hard. Children were being neglected, parents where separating, and cocaine was the king of any addict's world. People would sell their souls for a hit and Annie was no different.

Annie's body was now beginning to suffer the effects of crack. She was drying up. Even with the thought of losing her curves, and being unable to pull in any good tricks, she kept smoking crack. The glass pipe she sucked on was the only thing that mattered in life.

When Annie had finally reached the front of the line she placed a hundred dollar bill in the mail slot, and then a small brownbag with ten packets of crack were slipped out the slot to her. She darted away with her goodies. Within the hour she was in another addict's house soaring high as the clouds; but Annie was still on the clock.

Hood was on the lookout for his workers and called for two prostitutes he saw on the strip when he pulled up. They rushed over to his parked car.

"Destiny where is Annie," he said. The attractive redbone leaned up against his car and said, "Ain't seen her in a few hours." He was pissed. "Did she leave with a trick," he asked. "I don't think so, but I'm sure you probably know where she's been," Destiny said.

Hood rolled up his window and pulled off. He knew that Annie had been at the crack house. The drugs had a hold on her more than the beatings he had given her. Hood had put his foot in her ass over three times in the last two weeks, but she still disobeyed him. She was a thorn in

his side and he had to find a way to get his message across to her.

Chapter 62
December 9th, 1987

Doc sat in his chair and read The Philadelphia Inquirer. He had just read an article about the closing of the Penn-Hurst Mental Hospital. The State had finally got involved and uncovered the horrendous conditions the patients lived in, and the heinous acts they suffered at the hands of the staff. All four-hundred-and-sixty patients had to be transferred to other institutions for care, and many were deemed safe and allowed to return to society.

As he continued to read on he was shocked to finally hear news about his former master, Dr. Winston. The director was now a patient in a nearby assisted-living facility. Dr. Winston had survived the castration but he would never be the man he once was. One of the syringes Doc plunged inside of his neck left him paralyzed from the neck down, and he lost the ability to speak. The man who had victimized so many of his patients was now left to live a mundane existence; tormented by the daily reminder of his harsh reality.

A knock to his door got his attention and he went to his monitor to see who came to visit him. When he noticed it was two attractive females he rushed to his front door.

"Yes how can I help you," Doc said. "Are you that doctor that helps people around here," one of the women asked. "Yes. Why what's wrong," he said. "We need your help. It's a woman in the house down the street and she's bleeding all over the place," the one woman said. "Okay. Who are you guys," Doc asked, as he grabbed his medical bag. "My name is Pam and this is my friend Veronica. Please help her she's in pain," Pam said.

Doc followed the woman to the house where they said the woman was. He knew the house because it was a

popular crack house and some of his patients were often in that house. There was a crowd of people in the house surrounding the woman, and Doc had to push his way through to get to his patient. Once he cleared the path he was shocked to see Annie lying in a pool of blood clutching her stomach.

Doc rushed to Annie and she mumbled, "Randy, he killed our baby," as Doc looked down and saw that the blood was coming from her vagina. "What happened," Doc yelled out to the crowd. "Her pimp did it," someone said.

Doc picked up Annie and carried her out of the house and back to his home. She was hemorrhaging and had been bleeding for too long in her fragile condition. The trail of blood she left could clearly be seen by the onlookers as he carried her away. Her body was limp and she was showing no signs of life. Doc was devastated.

Chapter 63

Annie died on the operating table. She had internal bleeding and her body was in no shape to recover from the vicious attack she had received. She was dead and nothing Doc did could bring her back. He cried so intensely that he felt as if he would faint at any minute. He was filled with rage and sorrow; and nothing could take away the pain he felt.

He found the strength to clean up his Annie. He took an ultrasound of her belly and he thought about removing his child from her womb. He wanted to bury them separately but he decided the best thing would be for his child to stay inside of his mother and he'd bury them together.

Doc waited for the cover of darkness, and then he went into his fenced yard and began to dig a shallow grave. He had wrapped Annie in a white blanket and softly placed her inside of her grave. As the tears fell from his face her swore that was the last tear he'd ever shed. He had lost the only person on this earth that would ever be close to him and he swore off love. When he was finished covering their grave with the dirt, he was pleased to know his true love and child would be close to him; even if he would never see their faces again.

He stayed outside for hours as he looked up to the sky and cursed God, even though he didn't believe in a higher power.

"You took away everyone I loved. My mother, Annie, and my child. If you were real, I'd kill you! You can't be real and my mother spent her whole life wasting away praying to a thing that has no power to cure anyone! You killed your favorite servant you bastard! You're not real, and if you are show yourself! Show yourself to me and I'll show you God! Your world will fill my

vengeance, and they'll call to you and you won't answer. Each one I take I'll wait for you! Until then, I'll keep taking them until the day we meet," he raged on.

West Philadelphia

"It's crazy what happened to Annie," Veronica said. "Yeah it really is," Pamela said. "And just think, you wanted to follow in that chicks' footsteps," Pamela added. "Gurl, don't I know how lucky I am you talked me out of that shit. She fucked up her entire life, and that won't ever be me," Veronica said.

"Good, so who's the lucky guy tonight," Pamela asked. "His name is Mark," Veronica said, as she grabbed the new Gucci purse, he had bought her off her bed. "Mark? That's all the info you got on him, or is that all you're gonna tell me," Pamela asked, as she grinned. "Okay, since you need to know. He's a white guy, and he's twenty-eight, and he's got some money, plus he's the Assistant District Attorney," Veronica bragged.

Pamela sat on the bed and said, "Damn, you took my advice and ran with it, huh? Do that gurl!" Veronica looked at her and said, "Yes I did," as they began to laugh. "But seriously, I need this lifestyle. All my bills are paid and things couldn't be better. Most of my clients are married, so there are no strings. I provide a service and fulfill a fantasy, and they pay good money to keep me on the other side of their fence," Veronica continued.

"Just be careful. Money or not, there are some twisted people out in this world," Pamela said, as she looked out the window to check on her son, Face who was playing with his cousin, Reese. "You don't have to worry I take precautions. You see this," Veronica said flashing her .22. "Okay," Pamela said. "And Momma told me how to

152

use it, so I'm prepared to protect myself if I have to," Veronica said as the pair began to laugh.

"Pam, I want to ask you something," Veronica said. "Sure what is it," Pamela said. "I've been thinking about videotaping some of my clients. What do you think," Veronica said. "Well I don't know about that. I mean, what if it comes back to bite you in the ass," Pamela said. "Maybe you're right, but maybe one day they'll come in handy. I might get broke and need to blackmail a client or two," Veronica said, as Pamela burst out laughing. "Whatever you do, be smart about it," Pamela told her friend.

Twenty minutes later, Pam watched as Veronica got inside of a white BMW and drove off.

Chapter 64
1997
Ten Years Later

For a decade, Doc continued to live a double life. During the day he treated his patients but on his time he would kidnap, rape, and kill women whenever he got the chance. No one knew about his horrid ways. He kept to himself and never allowed anyone to get close to him, except for an eccentric and precocious seventeen-year old hustler named Face.

A few days out of the week, the youngster would stop by Doc's to pick up some sleeping pills. He had trouble sleeping, and Doc always found it odd that the young man thought so much he could never get his brain to rest. Face's grandmother was one of Doc's longtime patients, and he had watched the young man grow up right before his eyes.

One day Face and Doc were in his office talking. Face had brought his cousin Reese with him, and immediately, Reese didn't trust the doctor. He told Face he felt he was creepy and a crazy nut, which is what most people thought about Doc, but they still let him treat them. "So what is it my friend," Doc asked Face. "I need you to help us get rid of someone," Face told him. Doc grinned and said, "You mean kill someone." Reese gave Face the look as if he should not respond, but Face went on. "Yeah, kill somebody. I want this nigga dead for what he did to my mother," Face snapped, as he paced the floor. "And if I help you how will I know I can trust you with this secret," Doc asked. "We ain't no damn snitches," Reese yelled.

Face walked over to Doc and said, "Whatever you do for me will always be between us. My word is my bond and that's what I live on." Doc heard the sincerity in the

young man's words and saw his truth in his eyes. The young man was like no one he had ever met and he was very wise. The talks the two shared showed Doc that Face was highly intelligent, and he could outthink many people twice his age. Doc was inclined to help this young man.

"Okay I'll help you," Doc said. "Cool. I need you to be a part of my team," Face said. "Great. That sounds like it might be very interesting. Now who is it that you want me to get rid of," Doc asked. "His name is Hood. He raped my mother and killed my father. I want him dead," Face said.

Doc couldn't believe his ears. He had been trying to get to Hood for years but it was extremely hard for him to get his hands on him. Hoods was known throughout the city and had the protection of Detective Ron Perry as well as local street gangsters. He wasn't a respected man, he was feared; and people who had a grudge with him swallowed their pride and looked the other way.

"You know who he is," Face asked. "Yes. I heard of Hood," Doc said. "Well, we are going to kill his ass one day. Fuck his bitch ass," Reese said. "Face, you think you can get close to him," Doc asked curiously. "Yes I do. I know some of the same people that he knows. It's just a matter of time till we get a hold of him. I'm never going to rest until he's a dead man, and each day I look in the mirror, and see this scar on my face, I determined to get him even more. He's going to pay for what he did to my family," Face said.

"I'm going to help you my friend. Just stay focused on what you're doing out in the streets, and when the time is right you will have you revenge, and I will have mine. When you need me, I'm here, and if you get me Hood, I'll always be loyal to you. You'll have a friend in me for life," Doc said.

"What did Hood do to you," Face asked. "The man is a taker. He takes things that don't belong to him, and the two things that he took from me were my woman and my child. For that, he must pay with his life," Doc said. "Don't worry Doc, I'll get us close to him," Face said. "Good, and when you do his heart belongs to me," Doc said.

Chapter 65
March 3rd, 1999
Two Years Later

It had taken some time, but the day had come when Face was closer to the man who he had sworn revenge on. Face phoned Doc and said, "We got everything we need on Hood." Doc was excited. He was ready to go and he said, "You have Hood." Face responded, "No. Not yet. We have his main man, Killa-D and he's spilling his guts." Doc was eager to get closer to Hood and he said, "See you in a few," as he hung up the phone.

Forty-five minutes later, Reese pulled up in front of Doc's door and parked his Lexus. Doc was holding a large black leather bag that contained everything he would need for the upcoming job. He was excited as he entered the backseat of Reese's car, and they pulled of quickly.

"Do you think you can do it," Face asked Doc as he sat in the passenger seat. "I believe I can. I've been testing my skills on cats and dogs, and I've been very successful; well more than not," Doc said.

Reese drove and didn't say a word. No matter how many times he had been around Doc, the man always freaked him out. Every encounter he had with the doctor he learned a strange new detail about him. Face was in a trance as they drove, and then he instructed Reese to pull over.

"Listen, no matter what is ahead of us in this journey we are in this together. I have y'all back no matter what," Face said. "I agree we are a team and this will work out in our favor," Doc said. "Yeah, you're right. We are a team and as long as Hood pays for killing your pops and raping my aunt, and for taking Doc's family, we all good over here," Reese said, as they continued on their journey.

Chapter 66
Ardmore, PA

Within an hour, Reese parked his car behind a patch of tall trees. They were now in Ardmore, just a block away from Hood's beautiful home. Doc watched with growing excitement as Face and Reese checked out their loaded .9mm. Once the safeties were removed and the clips were fully loaded, they exited the car.

The sky was filled with darkness and the surrounding area was peaceful and quiet, except for the night sounds of frogs, crickets, and other night creatures. Hood's home was located in a secluded area, far away from all the other homes and no one saw the men as they approached his house. Before Face had killed Killa-D he had taken Hood's house key from him, and now he was going to pay the man that had scarred his face a surprise visit.

When they finally approached the front door, Face used the key to enter. The front door slowly opened, and they quietly stepped inside the elegant home. Face walked over to the Brink's Security System keypad, located on the wall, and entered the security code that Killa-D had given them. They wanted to be in and out before daylight arrived, and so far all was going well.

Nervousness filled each of their bodies as they quietly ascended the stairs. Face had waited over ten years for this day to finally come; the day when he would avenge his father's death and kill the man that had beat and raped his mother.

Face slowly turned the doorknob to the master suite, then pushed the door open and they all stepped inside the lavishly large bedroom. They looked at Hood and his wife who were snuggled up, peacefully sleeping in

their bed. With their guns aimed, they approached the bed. Face stared down at his sleeping prey with hate filled eyes.

"Hood," Face said, tapping him on the head with the tip of his gun. Hood quickly jumped up from his sleep, waking his wife Britney. "Don't say a fucking word," Face commanded. Hood and Britney both threw up their arms; scared, naked and confused. "You, get out the bed now," Face told Britney.

She nervously got out of bed and did what she was told. Reese and Doc watched as Britney lay her naked body down on the floor. They then quickly tied her up with thick silver duct tape. Hood sat back watching as they carried her body out of the room.

"Do you remember me," Face asked, his gun still aimed at Hood's head. Hood stared at Face shaking his head, "Yeah, I remember you. You're Pamela's son," he said. "Who did y'all get," Hood asked. "Your dead friend, Killa-D."

At that moment, Doc walked back into the room and said, "She's tied up with the two kids. Reese is in the back bedroom watching them." Hood looked at the strange white man and wondered what was going on. Something was telling him this was no regular robbery or kidnapping.

"Lay on your back," Face demanded. "Please, just don't hurt my wife and children," Hood begged. "I said lay on your fucking back!"

Hood looked into Face's stern eyes and did what he was told. As soon as he lay on his back, Doc started duct taping his arms to his side and his legs together.

"Please don't hurt my family," Hood pleaded, before Doc taped his mouth shut. Face stood over Hood's naked, exposed body, staring deep into his frightened eyes. He didn't say a word to him; his expression had said enough.

Doc sat next to Hood's body and emptied out his black leather bag. He grabbed a long syringe. Hood watched in total fear as Doc stuck an IV into his left arm. The clear plastic tube ran from the needle in Hood's arm, up and into the bag of clear liquid. Doc made a few adjustments, and then he injected a mysterious liquid into another tube that intersected the tube coming from the bag. Doc then removed a black marker from his bag and began drawing a line where he would begin his incision.

A strange warm feeling began to course through Hood's veins. His entire body began to feel heavy and numb. He could barely move his eyelids. At that moment, he realized he was completely paralyzed and yet he was totally aware of his surroundings.

After a few minutes, Doc looked up at Face and smiled. "Ready when you are," he said, with a mad chuckle bordering on insanity. "Are you sure this is gonna work," Face asked, glancing into the terrified eyes of Hood, his mortal enemy. "His body is completely numb and he is wide awake but he won't feel a thing. I promise." "But, will he know what is happening to him," Face asked anxiously.

Doc looked up at Face and a strange smile crossed his face and entered his eyes, "Oh yes, he'll know exactly what is happening. This could get a little gross. You may want to leave the room," Doc advised. "I'm fine," Face replied. Doc shrugged his shoulders and said, "Okay."

"Just let me know when he is about to die," Face said. "You got it, Face," Doc said, holding his scalpel poised and ready.

Moments later, Face stood back in awe of what he was witnessing. Doc carefully and methodically cut through bones, muscle, and cartilage; as he surgically opened Hood's chest cavity.

Forty-five minutes had passed when Doc looked up at Face and said, "Get the jar." Face grabbed the large glass jar off of the floor and held it out. Doc reached into Hood's chest cavity and quickly removed the large pumping organ. His bloody hands rose upwards so Hood could see what he was holding. With complete awareness, Hood watched as his heart was held up before his eyes.

"You've got less than ten seconds," Doc said, placing the spastic muscle into the jar. Hood looked on in complete horror as Face aimed his gun directly between his eyes and without hesitation squeezed the trigger, killing Hood instantly. With his eyes engulfed with tears, Face turned and left the bedroom.

When Face walked into the back bedroom, Britney, Robbie, and Arianna were seated against the wall. They were all tied up in duct tape, with white pillowcases over their heads. Reese was standing over them with his pistol in his hand.

"Y'all take care of everything," Reese asked. "It's done," Face replied, nodding his head. "You know this bitch is a cop, right," Reese asked. "Go ahead and get it over with," Face said. Reese walked up to Britney's naked body and pointed his gun at her head.
POP!!!
He shot her once in the head and watched as her body slumped over to the side.

"What about the two kids," Reese asked, as he walked over to them and aimed his pistol at them. After a thoughtful sigh, Face said, "No, leave them alone. I got who I came for."

Reese placed his pistol under his t-shirt and followed Face out of the bedroom, leaving the two terrified children crying into their duct taped mouths.

Although they couldn't see they knew their mother lay dead only a few feet away.

Doc was waiting for them out in the hallway. He was carrying his bag of medical instruments with the large jar containing Hood's heart.

"Our job is done. Let's get out of here," Face said, as they started walking toward the stairs. Doc stopped and said, "Y'all fellas wait for me downstairs. I'll be another minute or so."

Face and Reese looked at Doc's strange expression. "Is everything alright, Doc," Face asked.
"Everything is fine. I just need a minute to take care of something," Doc said. "Okay, we'll be downstairs," Face said, and then he and Reese turned and walked away.

"What's up with Doc," Reese asked, as they walked down the stairs. "I don't know and I'm afraid to find out," Face said, as he smiled and sat on the arm of the sofa. Reese nodded and smiled in agreement. They both knew Doc was a very strange motherfucker.

"Oh, shit," Face said. "What is it," Reese asked. "We forgot the money," Face said. He and Reese jumped up and ran back up the stairs into the master suite.

The sight of Hood's mutilated body, along with the overwhelming smell of blood had them on the verge of vomiting. Face opened the closet door and Reese followed him inside. They saw two large black suitcases on the top shelf. They each reached up and grabbed one of the suitcases. Face sat his on the floor and unzipped it. Neat stacks of hundred-dollar bills stared him in the face. It was the most money either of them had ever seen.

"Damn! Killa-D was right again," Reese laughed. They each carried one of the heavy suitcases out of the bedroom and closed the door behind them. The latex surgical gloves they had all been wearing prevented them from leaving any fingerprints behind.

They stood in the hallway waiting for Doc. He was still in the back bedroom with the two kids and Britney's corpse.

"Come on, let's go see what's taking Doc so long," Face said. They sat their suitcases down and started walking toward the back bedroom. When they approached the closed door, they heard a loud grunting sound coming from the other side. When Face turned the doorknob and pushed the door open, he and Reese stood there in total shock. They couldn't believe their eyes. Doc was lying on top of Britney's naked corpse. His pants were around his knees and he was having sex with her dead body. Doc was engaged in the same heinous act that had gotten him kicked out of medical school and banned from his profession. Doc quickly stood up and pulled up his pants. He was so embarrassed to be caught, again!

While they all walked out of the front door, carrying two suitcases filled with money, and a jar filled with a human heart, neither of them said a word. The job they had come to do was completed and they had all gotten their revenge and then some.

Once they were inside of the car, Face looked at Doc and said, "What was done in that house will always stay between us. Not one of us in this car is perfect and none of us is fit to judge the other." Doc felt relieved by the young man's words and after shaking Face's hand he sat back and enjoyed his ride home; as he held the jar with Hood's heart in his hand.

When Reese dropped Doc off, he said goodbye to his two friends and rushed into his backyard. He fell onto his knees and kissed the cold ground where his beloved Annie was buried.

"I got him, Annie. He's gone now," he whispered. Doc could finally smile. Killing Hood had ended a saga and brought him some peace. He had lost his mother, his

child, and his sweet Annie, but he was not alone. He had a friend that he could trust, one that wouldn't judge him and allowed him to do the things that made him tick. Doc was now a part of Face's organization and the doctor would have many more stories to tell.

KING

JIMMY DASAINT

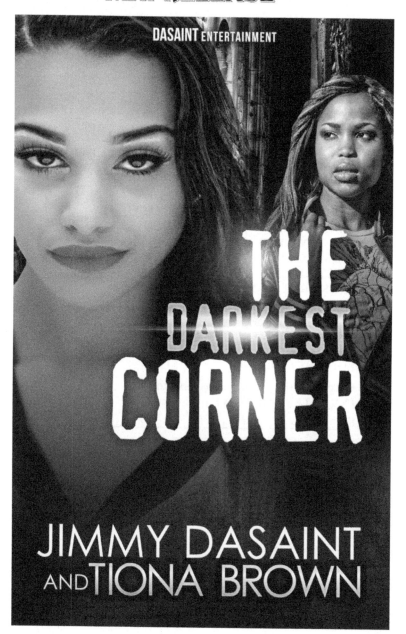

DASAINT ENTERTAINMENT

THE DARKEST CORNER

JIMMY DASAINT
AND TIONA BROWN

DASAINT ENTERTAINMENT ORDER FORM

Please visit www.dasaintentertainment.com to place online orders.

You can also fill out this form and send it to:

DASAINT ENTERTAINMENT
PO BOX 97
BALA CYNWYD, PA 19004

TITLE	PRICE	QTY
BLACK SCARFACE	$15.00	_____
BLACK SCARFACE II	$15.00	_____
BLACK SCARFACE III	$15.00	_____
BLACK SCARFACE IV	$15.00	_____
DOC	$15.00	_____
YOUNG RICH & DANGEROUS	$15.00	_____
WHAT EVERY WOMAN WANTS	$15.00	_____
THE UNDERWORLD	$15.00	_____
A ROSE AMONG THORNS	$15.00	_____
A ROSE AMONG THORNS II	$15.00	_____
CONTRACT KILLER	$15.00	_____
MONEY DESIRES & REGRETS	$15.00	_____
ON EVERYTHING I LOVE	$15.00	_____
WHO	$15.00	_____
AIN'T NO SUNSHINE	$15.00	_____
SEX SLAVE	$15.00	_____
THE DARKEST CORNER	$15.00	_____

Make Checks or Money Orders payable to:
DASAINT ENTERTAINMENT

NAME: _____

ADDRESS: _____

_____

CITY: _____ STATE: _____
ZIP:_____ PHONE:_____

PRISON ID NUMBER_____

$3.50 per item for Shipping and Handling
($4.95 per item for Expedited Shipping)

WE SHIP TO PRISONS!!!

Made in the USA
Las Vegas, NV
01 April 2022

46698405R00095